THE RATTLING CAT

A tale of smuggling in the eighteenth
century on the Kentish coast

The Rattling Cat

Published by The Conrad Press in the United Kingdom 2021

Tel: +44(0)1227 472 874
www.theconradpress.com
info@theconradpress.com

ISBN 978-1-914913-14-3

Typesetting and Cover Design by: Charlotte Mouncey, www.bookstyle.co.uk
The Conrad Press logo was designed by Maria Priestley.

Printed and bound in Great Britain by Clays Ltd, Elcograf S.p.A.

THE RATTLING CAT

A tale of smuggling in the eighteenth
century on the Kentish coast

SIMON GREGORY

with illustrations by Susan Beresford

For Michael, Susan,
Victoria and Hannah.

My oldest friends in teaching

Contents

BONES

BONES pulled up the high collar of his greatcoat to protect himself against the biting cold.

His aged bay mare shuffled beneath him, sensing the mounting tension as he waited impatiently for the approach of the post coach along the Deale - Dover Road. Droplets of moisture fell from the damp branches of the bare trees. They wormed their way under the multi-layered capes and wriggled behind the elderly highwayman's scrawny neck.

Drip. Drip. . Drip. . .

He shivered. He yawned. He was frozen to the marrow! This, despite the fact that his skeletal frame was muffled up to his treble chin in thick winter clothes. His greatcoat had been stolen from a magistrate, his brimmed hat from a farmer, his spotted neckerchief from a parson and his riding boots from a lord. Travellers, all, along this twisting coastal road in a remote corner of south-east Kent. Only Bones' double-barrelled pistol - ready cocked with powder primed in the pan - had been purchased legally (admittedly with money forcibly surrendered by his frightened victims) from a disreputable gunsmith.

Oxney Bottom, where our 'gentleman of the road' had purposely stationed himself, was reputedly haunted. There were persistent tales of a mysterious grey lady who appeared and disappeared at will on her forlorn way through the woods to the ruined chapel of derelict Oxney Court. The place was definitely eerie. Over the muddy highway the tops of tall trees clasped together like the hands of a vindictive witch while from the overgrown verges mist bellowed like smoke from her steaming cauldron. The crisp, night air had formed a natural phenomenon in the pocket of the lonely hills, famed locally as a 'Frost Hollow'.

Yet, although the scene appeared ghostly, the danger was real and present. The wily highwayman had chosen his position carefully. He knew from experience that the unwary coachman would struggle to steady his horses down the slippery slope, pause at the bottom for the guard to jump down and disengage the drag shoe from the nearside rear wheel that acted as a brake, then whip up his team for them to scale the tortuous incline ahead. When the horses reached the top of the opposite hill, exhausted after their strenuous climb, it would be the perfect time to reveal himself from his place of concealment and halt the post coach.

Bones squinted through his borrowed gold-rimmed spectacles to search for the headlamps through the veil of mist while his mare pricked her ears to listen for the drumming of the horses' hooves. After a while, she raised her head slightly, whinnied softly and scraped a front hoof, alerting her master of the approach of the post coach now rattling at speed through Oxney Bottom. Suddenly, it rose through the frost like a phantom - clouds of steam rising from the flanks of the mettlesome horses - as it strained to reach the brow of the hill. This was the moment to strike!

Bones spurred his mare into action. He emerged from his hiding place, rode towards the centre of the road and pointed his pistol straight ahead at the lumbering post coach. The leading horses shied at the apparition and the coachman tightened his reins to prevent the whole team from bolting. The post coach skidded and slithered, then slewed to a halt.

'Stand and deliver!'

Curiously, Bones' threatening command was met with derision. The coachman betrayed neither surprise nor fear. The guard, perched precariously in his rumble seat at the rear, didn't even trouble to reach into the sword box at his feet for a weapon.

'What have you got for me tonight, Coachie?' growled the highwayman.

'Take a look for yourself, Mr Bones,' rejoined the coachman, haughtily from his high perch.

But the highwayman did not wait for this ironic invitation. He spun his revolver round and with its heavy butt ripped open the leather shutters that protected the small opening in the door panel. He poked his head through and peered inside the dark interior of the post coach. The cold air rushed in with a sting of icy mist. Framed in the centre of the jagged aperture, Bones looked for all the world like a hoary Jack Frost.

Sitting bolt upright on the damp leather seat in the far corner facing the horses was a solitary occupant. . . a terrified small boy. Both his hands grasped the safety strap above the nearside window while his feet struggled to reach the pitted floor. His startled eyes peered out from behind the high collar of his powder blue peacoat. He much resembled a drowning man about to disappear for the third and final time beneath the unruly waves.

In London, much earlier that chill, late autumn day, Miles' anxious mother had escorted her son to the 'Golden Cross', the premier coaching inn at Charing Cross. This was a glorious confection of galleries, passages, staircases and stables (mostly underground) leading from a crowded courtyard, all under the control of an officious head porter. There she placed him in the care of the chirpy coachman as his packed stagecoach prepared to leave on its tortuous journey across Kent.

The yet dark, crowded courtyard came alive with the heavy rumble of carts and drays, the sound of pattens clattering on cobbles, the bawling of newsmen, milkmen and muffin men, plying their wares to prospective passengers. There was the ceaseless whooping and jumble from the arrival and departure of coaches from different parts of the kingdom: 'Atlas' leaving for its tortuous journey to Bath: 'Comet' arriving in record time from Oxford.

Fussily, she helped her son climb the folding iron steps into the upholstered interior and insisted he found a seat facing the horses where he would then be less likely to vomit from the swaying of the coach. (After all, even at his young age, he was still required to pay the full fare). She handed him his canvas bag containing his personal possessions before going to triple check his hastily packed trunk stowed in the wide wicker basket at the rear. There the scarlet coated guard, who was mightily skilled in the use of firearms, had already positioned himself on his precariously high seat. Beneath him the coach's name was inscribed in bold crimson and gold letters onto its black and maroon livery: 'THE MAGNET'.

The horn sounded shrilly for departure. The eager postillion mounted the nearside horse of the front pair and signalled his readiness. The coachman raised his hat politely to his passengers and climbed onto his hard box seat where the groom handed him his waybill along with the reins for the nearest four matching bays. A crack of his whip, a stamp of his boot and the team of six strong horses strained on their collars, jolting the heavy coach on its steel springs. Shoed hooves and iron rims clattered over the cobbled innyard. As the coach approached the low brick archway the coachman cried: 'Heads, heads, take care of your heads!' This was to warn less fortunate passengers travelling outside, wrapped tightly in their blankets, scarves and shawls, to either duck or be beheaded at the very start of their journey.

The boy's mother cheerily waved her handkerchief as the coach turned sharply out of the gates and onto the high road. Then she employed it discreetly to dab tears from her eyes.

She adjusted the prettily ribboned straw bonnet to hide her despondent face and then disappeared among the newspaper, orange and pie sellers to look for her waiting carriage which would take her swiftly home to the riverside village of Chiswick. The family's spaniel, Lucy, accompanying her was confused at seeing her young master leave so abruptly and kept looking up at her mistress in vain for reassurance that all was well.

Squashed between a jovial sailor clutching his diddy box and a portly farmer's wife balancing a china ewer and basin on her lap, there was precious little room for the boy to manoeuvre. At least their ample weight shielded him from the constant swaying and lurching of the coach. It spanked across the barren countryside at around ten or twelve miles an hour. They paused once or twice at intermittent crossroads to pick up further passengers who clambered on top. But the driver always made up his top speed so that customers outside village inns swore that they could set their watches by this reliable coachman who they referred to, simply, as: 'Dover'.

Miles was intrigued, as he struggled to bend forward, to catch fleeting glimpses through the restricted coach windows of landmarks - Rochester Castle and Canterbury Cathedral. He was amused by the brace of partridges the countrywoman had slung over the lamp brackets that appeared to take flight as they swung outwards whenever the coach swerved round corners. Opposite him sat a thin, nervous woman, sipping bitters and nibbling bread to settle her stomach. Perhaps she was contemplating that before she attempted this tiresome journey, she ought to have made out her will?

Conversation was restricted as the travellers, even in that confined space, were forced to shout to each other to make themselves heard above the racket of the carriage wheels. They competed to warm their feet on the iron brazier filled with hot coals and their hands with the shared blankets draped across their knees. Miles entertained himself by counting the milestones and reading the direction posts as they whizzed by. . .

Earlier, there had been only one real delay - apart from the brief stops at frequent intervals to change horses while the passengers snatched refreshment - when the four male occupants were required to leave the comfort of their own vehicle to help right the faster night mail coach travelling in the opposite direction - 'up' rather than 'down' from London - which had skidded into a patch of deep mud.

The troubled mail coach bore the royal scarlet, maroon and black livery with scarlet wheels. The royal arms were emblazoned on the door panel and the royal cipher on the foreboot: 'G. III R'. Its guard-in-chief, who wore a scarlet and gold livery, sat on the single rearmost seat with the mailbags stored in a locker directly under his feet. He had already abandoned the coachman along with his stranded passengers and commandeered the cock horse to deliver those valuable mailbags to the London Post Office. He also made sure he took with him the brace of pistols leaving only the blunderbuss with the coachman to defend himself against robbers that might confront him once he resumed his journey.

As dusk approached, Miles' stagecoach drew to a halt on the last lap of its journey and pulled up at Dover's chief hostelry, 'The Ship'. The head porter uncoupled the horses and led them to their stables where they were rubbed down against the freezing cold. The passengers, complaining they had been jolted 'black and blue', disbursed into the shadows and went about their business - to farm, to ship, to the office or to their homes. The obliging long-stage coachmen, true to his promise, directed his small charge with his minimal luggage onto the night post coach and four, already waiting at its station. This would convey him up the steep 'zig zag' hill (which he would be required to walk) adjacent to the clifftop Norman castle and along the eight miles winding high road to his final destination, the town and port of Deale.

This new coachman was Goggins. A cheerful character, he did not seem to mind - at least he never once showed it - that his single fare was a mere boy. After all, the lad although slightly dishevelled from his long journey looked a 'proper gentleman'.

He displayed polished manners; he spoke with polite assurance. Goggins would take the same care of him as though his coach was brimful of lords and ladies.

Indeed, although his post coach was a veteran vehicle, he treated it with the same respect he did his passengers. A man of immense pride, Goggins, huddled in his many caped 'benjamin' driving coat, declined to employ inferior horses, perhaps disfigured by accidents or poor conformation, at night time. Further, he took satisfaction in the fact that, unlike long distance coachmen, he had developed the enviable skill of driving all his horses individually, four in hand. Confidently, he manipulated the separate 'ribbons', passing them deftly between the fingers of his left hand, while holding the long-handled whip, pointing it precisely diagonally forward, in his right. After a few warming drinks, he would boast he could swipe a fly off the arse of the cock horse with just one flick. (At times, he was sorely tempted to strike off complaining passengers' hats!)

A further source of his great pride was the fact that, even at his advanced age, he had acquired a young sweetheart. She had presented him with a nosegay of wintersweet to pin to his greatcoat, its pungent scent a poignant reminder of her true love. Goggins had found substance in the phrase: 'the romance of the road'.

But now, roused from his reveries, Goggins had to face the practicalities of the way ahead. He was fast approaching Oxney Bottom. A notorious, dangerous stretch, it veered sharply to the right among dense woods while descending, at the same time, an alarmingly steep valley. He would need to take great care not to corner too quickly.

Time now to pause for the guard to jump down and apply the drag shoe to the rear wheels. This would prevent the heavy body of the post coach from crashing into the nearest pair of horses as it made its precarious descent. Goggins' expertise would be required to pass control from these equine 'wheelers' as they steadied his vehicle when it slid down the hill and then pass it over to the 'leaders' as it sped up the far side. Additional danger was presented by that pocket of frost lying stagnant in the deep hollow. Temporarily, he would be driving blind.

To Miles, the day had already been the start of a great adventure. An imaginative boy, he longed for the excitement that lay ahead in the ancient seaport. It would take his mind off recent family concerns. But, awakened sharply from his dreams, he realised at once that the rugged face of the elderly highwayman, whose features were illuminated by moonlight, was tangible and threatening. And that both barrels of his pistol were pointing directly at his forehead.

By now, the highwayman had prized open the door and was peeping into the musty coach. Man and boy came face to face. Forever afterwards, Miles would recall every despicable feature: the cruel curve of his top lip, the hairy wart on the side of his prominent nose. Bones' teeth were like lichen encrusted tombstones; his foul breath smelled like a cockle swamp. There were splashes of food stains - 'canteen medals' - all down the front of his worn greatcoat.

Bones' eyes, although dimmed with age, searched intensely every inch of Miles' apparel for valuables. There were no signs of rings, brooches, stock buckle nor pocket watch.

Alas, one tiny gesture gave the game away. The boy nervously fingered something shiny concealed about his neck. It was an oval locket on a gold chain containing his father's miniature portrait with a lock of his hair. At that moment, so early into his escapade, he knew he was about to lose his most precious possession.

Like a lightning strike from a cobra, Bones snatched at the chain which instantly snapped in two.

Turning it over in his knurled hands he examined his rare find. He slammed the door shut with his bony elbow while his greedy mouth slobbered his satisfaction. He was so engrossed in gloating over his spoil that he failed to register the sarcasm in the praise offered by the coachman.

'You've done well there, Mr Bones. Not any boy, you understand. Lew, the landlord's nephew. Down from London for a spell at the seaside.'

Gathering the reins, Goggins seized the opportunity to whip up his horses and continue his short journey. There was only a slight pause as the slackness of the tack was taken up before that exhilarating jolt into movement, sending small stones spinning like spent shot from under the heavy iron rimmed wheels.

The wind whistled through the splintered shutters of the rumbling coach. Miles swayed on the leather buttoned seat now mantled with frost. He hung his head in shame for, although the innocent victim of a robbery, he felt as though he had betrayed his family's trust. Distraught, distressed, degraded. . . and in the deepest despair, he was unprepared for the second shock of that fateful evening.

Before the post coach had time to gain speed, Miles' gold locket and chain were hurled through the torn aperture where they landed on the straw strewn floor.

The post coach whisked along the short stretch of coastal road stopping only to pay the toll at the spiked gate on the landward side of Deale Castle. The toll keeper was a lazy fellow, reluctant to leave the warmth and comfort of his wooden shelter to unlock the gate for a public vehicle. His attitude fueled the resentment that Goggins held for the competing mail coaches that not only had priority on the roads but were excused from paying the expensive tolls. He considered them a perfect nuisance, their guards arrogantly blowing their horn to warn of their approach, scattering pedestrians, herds of cattle and droves of sheep in busy market towns across Kent.

Deale had been garrisoned immediately upon the commencement of the French Wars.

Miles peered through the torn window of the coach and was rewarded with his first glimpse of France. Lights from the twin ports of Calais and Boulogne were perfectly visible for they were just twenty or so miles across the narrowest section of the English Channel. Even at this late hour there was movement of troops along this vulnerable stretch of coastline, so close to the Continent. There was reliable intelligence that France was preparing for invasion after its republican government had declared war on Great Britain.

Deale was renowned for three castles built by King Harry the Eighth when he, too, feared attack from both Catholic France and Spain after his callous divorce of his first wife, Queen Katherine, from Aragon. The trio of fortresses were positioned at precisely one mile distant along the coast - Walmer, Deale and Sandown - although all three had fallen into alarming decay. They were being hastily repaired to billet troops on the orders of William Pitt, Britain's youngest Prime Minister, who, as Lord Warden of the Cinque Ports, resided frequently at Walmer Castle. Pitt had declared his determination - even if it meant higher taxation for every citizen in the country - to repel invasion by the hostile French.

After the French Revolution and the execution of their

despised King and Queen, the republican government had declared war on Britain. Immediately, Pitt had ordered the construction of tremendous barracks at Walmer for the British Army. They were intended to accommodate both infantry and cavalry but, although the stabling was almost complete, the living quarters were far from habitable. Instead, the first troops to be drafted in - and they were the prestigious 15th Light (or King's) Dragoons - had been forced to find temporary billets in outlying farms, barns and stables.

And now the post coach rattled and rumbled past the King's Navy Yard. Miles, sitting bolt upright, was alert to its complexity on the seaward side of Deale. Behind high walls with spiked gates was the profusion of naval offices, boatsheds, warehouses, victualling stores, sail lofts, single and double slip-ways, constructed so high that, it was claimed, a gentleman might walk underneath them without removing his hat!

Prominent among the profusion of buildings was the revolutionary new shutter telegraph. Silhouetted by the full moon, it towered above the roof of the Port Admiral's residence.

The telegraph was the first in a dozen overland stations that connected with the Admiralty in Whitehall. By means of an ingenious scheme of rotating shutters, simple coded messages - 'fleet arrived', 'enemy sighted' - might be communicated in a matter of minutes from Deale to London. Miles was keen to see this contraption operating in daylight as he heard it was universally hailed as 'the phenomenon of the age'.

Goggins slowed his horses to a gentle trot as his post coach turned into the boatmen's quarter with its warren of intriguing streets and beguiling alleys at Deale's North End. All the modest houses there, with their intriguing arrangements of doors, windows, roofs and chimneys, huddled together against the elements. They turned this way and that, rising above the narrow roads, appearing to be leaning into each other. . . sharing confidences, whispering secrets, conspiring against intruders.

Finally, the post coach bowled up at the 'Noah's Ark' Inn.

This was a brooding red brick building, two storeys high, identifiable by its wall mounted aleboards, located halfway along meandering Middle Street. There were windows galore on the top two floors and a pair of tall chimneys at opposite ends of the peg tiled roof, from one of which only smoke corkscrewed lazily into the clear night sky. Directly above the wide central doorway hung a pictorial innsign. This depicted the biblical story of animals meandering in pairs towards the mighty wooden ark that stood, incongruously, on dry land. The sign swung slightly in the light breeze which appeared to rock the bulky ark into motion, almost as if to alert the animals who dawdled to make haste or be trapped by the imminent deluge.

Miles was helped down the single step and handed his luggage. Not being a coaching inn, 'Noah's Ark' provided no stabling and therefore there was an absence of stableboys, ostlers or grooms to offer him further assistance. Goggins clambered back onto his hard seat and his dispirited horses plodded onwards to his command. His concern now was for them to be rested and baited. Coach and horses turned inland and were soon swallowed up in the night. . . almost as though they had never been.

All Miles had to do now was to pluck up courage to enter the inn. He was then confronted by a daunting dark passage with a choice of rooms - left or right - entered through swing doors, each with tiny oval windows at head height. He had now to decide which door to open. The obvious choice was the one exuding roisterous music and raucous laughter, the tap room. He touched the retrieved locket with its broken chain in his waistcoat pocket with his numb fingers for luck before making his decision. Dragging his small trunk and gripping his canvas bag tightly against his chest, almost as a protective shield, he elbowed open a door, the one to the right.

Despite the overwhelming smell of beer and tar, the atmosphere was unexpectedly bright and cheerful. The room was long and low with an uneven flagstone floor. There was a wide stone hearth with a crackling driftwood fire and a deep brick inglenook with settle seats halfway along one side. There was a large wall mounted tavern clock with a broad painted dial, an exposed pendulum and a single hand to indicate the hours. Huge carved mirrors made the room appear deceptively wide; glass smoke bells collecting fumes hung from the ancient rafters and swags of sweet, heady dried hops twisted around the sturdy blackened beams. Yet the flickering lights from the candles, oil lamps and log fire failed to disguise the cracked walls, bowed ceiling and tired chocolate brown and bottle green paintwork.

There was a pervading reek of stale tobacco and a lingering taste of sour beer. There was a chattering of servants and a clattering of plates; there was a clanking of large pots and a chinking of small change; there was a crunching of sea boots and a crackling of scorched logs. Above all, there was an overpowering atmosphere of unwashed bodies and damp clothes.

Smoke went everywhere but up the chimney. Yet through the convivial fug Miles could discern the animated company. Men smoked pipes, played dice, studied newsheets or sang songs to the accompaniment of a fiddle and a concertina. These were hardy folk in the main with weather worn faces that betrayed a tough life, earning their livelihood from the turbulent sea. Here was a mixture of pilots and pursers, boatbuilders and sailmakers, masters and mariners. An attractive young barmaid with black curly hair moved deftly among these rough, rude fellows, replenishing their pewter tankards which the distrustful landlord had chained to the tables.

Set apart was a small party of wealthier travellers who sat in a circle around the fireside. They had arrived from London on a previous coach, expecting to board their ship in the Downs, that famous anchorage off Deale. Becalmed, their sailing ship could not depart because of the lack of wind and thus their voyage was delayed indefinitely. They had resigned themselves to staying at the inn for several days, perhaps weeks or even months, until a strong northerly wind could carry their ship down Channel and onwards to remote corners of the world. They were the most valued customers whose purses would be stretched as they paid dearly for board and lodgings at the 'Ark'. Holding court, and regaling them with hearty tales of the sea, was mine host, Miles' uncle, Lew Bristowe.

Lew was a slight character with a slender frame. He had a tanned face, a hooked nose and a mat of unkempt dark hair. His slow smile revealed a set of sharp, chipped teeth that gave him a lean and hungry look, much like a certain story-book wolf. For the time being, he was relaxing with his guests, perched on the arm of the settle with one booted foot on the raised hearth and a half-filled glass of ale in his brutal hand. As the door swung open, he turned and viewed the newcomer with curiosity and contempt.

The merriment had ceased abruptly the moment the timid

boy appeared. Uncle Lew turned to greet his young relative. He declined to shake his hand but merely nodded his head in recognition. As he towered above him, he gave that measured smile while his jet black eyes remained cold and menacing. 'My nephew, Miles,' he announced flatly, kicking a fallen log back into the blazing fire. His customers relaxed and continued their chatter. The musicians resumed their playing. Miles was left standing, confused, conspicuous, uncomfortable.

Through the crowd, appeared Aunt Gwen. Miles recognised her at once although he had never before seen her. She was the mirror image, though slightly older, of her sister, his adored mother. She had the same golden locks, the same freckles, the same dainty nose. . . and the same smile, warm and welcoming. Fussily, just like his mother, she embraced her nephew. She took off his hat and ruffled his hair. She held him at arms length and eyed him keenly. Then made a snap decision. 'My boy, you must be hungry!'

Aunt Gwen steered him towards a corner of the crowded room. She cleared a trestle table and magicked up a tablecloth. She recalled the cook to prepare a late meal, irrespective of the cost of burning candles, and sat the boy down to enjoy a rare feast. Sweet and savoury served together. From nowhere appeared a tureen of fish soup, a beefsteak and oyster pudding, roasted eggs, buttered crabs, hog pie, a dish of stewed eels, trenchers of cheeses with yellow pickles and platters of carved meats, the slices arranged like playing cards dealt at a gaming table.

Miles had rarely eaten in public - he dined privately in his schoolroom with his tutor - and meals at roadside inns were frowned upon by his parents. It was a novelty, too, to eat food that was piping hot. At home, they were cooked in the vast kitchens and brought to the table by servants via a tortuous route, which meant invariably they were served lukewarm. Hot meals were a sign of poverty being served directly from a flaming fire.

Reaching for his drawstring bag he produced a French ivory handled silver knife and fork wrapped up in a lawn linen kerchief. He used this to wipe his own cutlery clean before tucking it into his collar to protect the front of his weskit. He ate slowly and delicately, conscious that all eyes in the room were directed once more upon him. Conversation lowered. Finishing his main repast, he turned his plate over and ate plum pudding from its upturned bowl. He had been careful each time to leave something on the side of his plate rather gobble it all up. A matter of instilled politeness.

The customers were absorbed. They had never seen anyone, let alone a mere boy, eat with such delicacy. It was as if he came from another world.

'Your neffew is most re-fined.'

'Who does he take after, Lew?'

'He acts like one of the gentry!'

'Maybe he is. . . of a sorts,' Lew scoffed. 'That's if you can call any Frenchie a *gentleman*.'

He reached above the high counter for some flinty, grey wine glasses which he wiped clean with a vengeance. 'His father's away, salvaging his estates in southern France.' He spat on a glass and rubbed it with a stained cloth. 'With luck, they'll keep him there and then he can take his whole family with him. But for the present I've been left with another mouth to feed.' He scowled. 'One with a big appetite, it seems.'

Disgruntled, he re-joined the frustrated travellers. He

produced a long-nosed bottle of rich, ruby wine, bit off the cork and spat it aside before sharing it with his favoured guests at the fireside.

'Take no notice, lad,' reassured Aunt Gwen. She sat with her arms folded over the opposite end of the table, watching with approval his every mouthful. She leaned over and poured him a small beer. 'This should warm the cockles.' She smiled as he took a manly swig. 'You could have eaten in the public room across the passage but it's far too cold in there. The fire isn't lit all winter, Lord knows why.' She offered him fruit. 'When you've finished, I'll show you to your room.'

A potboy appeared from nowhere to take charge of Miles' luggage. He disappeared with it through a far door, struggling with its weight, because of his pronounced limp. Aunt Gwen, fussing still, reached for his overcoat, casually draped over the back of his chair. 'Let him be,' growled Uncle Lew over his shoulder. 'He must learn to be independent. Otherwise, he'll never make a boatman. Don't mollycoddle the boy!'

But the boy did not need any 'mollycoddling'. The son of the man who once dared to defend his reputation in a duel had undeniably inherited his courage. At his surprise declaration, the whole company was first startled, then rocked on their chairs, stamped with their boots and banged on the table with their tankards, roaring with laughter.

'Leave that!', Miles commanded. And tugging his arm into a sleeve he announced, 'I'm off to look for smugglers!'

Spellbound, Miles stared at the panorama that now presented itself before him. It was beautiful and inspiring.

Ahead lay that that vast expanse of deep water known as the Downs crowded with Royal Navy and Merchant sailing ships, riding safely at anchor. Skeletal masts were silhouetted on the horizon against the the bold winter's moon. Shards of silver light played on the gentle waves, lapping rhythmically on the sparkling shingle. There was little activity apart from a few rowing boats plying from shore to ship and ship to shore.

The whole scene, thought Miles, resembled a painted glass slide or 'still' of a magic lantern that he recalled once presented by an itinerant showman in a barn on his father's estate as a welcome entertainment for his family and workers one chill harvest evening.

An array of distant twinkling lights came from ships' lanterns, marker buoys and, more intensely, the recently installed northern lightvessel indicating that hidden menace, the Goodwin Sands. Unfathomable to this inquisitive young gentleman, they indicated to an experienced navigator, when consulting his charts, the infinite dangers and obstacles of this narrowest stretch of the overcrowded seaway, the English Channel.

By contrast to the polluted sky with which Miles was familiar in London, the night sky over the Downs was brilliantly illuminated by myriad stars and planets. He recalled the time his father had taken him in their private travelling chariot to Primrose Hill to study the clear evening sky high over the City. From that time onwards he was able to identify several of the major constellations. Here, in the south, Miles observed Orion wielding his sword drawn from his starry belt like a warrior tipsy with triumph. And in the north the Plough that looked, Miles considered, more like a saucepan balancing comically on its handle. He knew that it pointed to the North Star by which mariners since time immemorial steered. But which one was it? A true landsman, Miles remained perplexed.

Turning to view the whole length of the lonely beach Miles observed the scattered clusters of boatmen's sheds, look outposts, wooden capstans and iron winches, landing stages and timber jetties. Try as hard as he might, Miles could discern little movement on the shore that might indicate the nefarious activities of the Midnight Men. There was not so much as one single suspicious shadow along that long, exposed foreshore.

Overhead, the rising moon, at the full, continued to climb on its predetermined arc over the Channel. It moved slowly and seductively, with its sly smile, revealing, as if by sleight of hand, a strip of land in the far distant south. This was the opposite coast where a hostile army, Miles had been warned, threatened invasion.

Before Miles' very eyes this sovereign moon turned from polished silver to rose gold, transformed, it would seem, by the artifice of an invisible conjurer. His dubious motive, it might be guessed, was to entice humble Deale boatmen - desperate to improve their harsh seafaring lifestyle - to risk the law and perhaps even their lives in search of contraband by venturing over the still water to France.

2

BOATHOUSE

MILES awoke to the promise of an exciting new day.
He had been far too tired the night before to take
stock of the differences between his own spacious bedroom
and the cramped attic he had been allocated for the next few
weeks. At home, his soft feather bed would have been made
up with crisp linen sheets, his lace pillows scented with laven-
der while the candle on his bedside table would have been
pure beeswax. The housemaid would have first run a copper
warming pan filled with live coals under the laundered sheets
to take off the chill before he slipped contentedly into his
enveloping bed.

In the morning the pretty housemaid would light a fire in
his bedroom, bring him a jug of steaming hot water for his
ablutions and place a breakfast tray on a table by the window
before he even considered rising from his slumbers. Only when
he was ready would he stroll over to the schoolroom and begin
the day's lessons after first remembering to enquire politely after
his parents' health. How things change! Here, he was directed
over to the yard where he had a strip wash under the hand
pump before returning to the taproom for his meagre breakfast
of bread, cheese and ale.

A proud young gentleman, Miles was reflecting just how cosseted he was by his doting family back in London. Even his shoes would have been polished by a man servant when he left them overnight outside his bedroom door. He was struggling to put them on and thinking why on earth did shoemakers not think to make them left or right, instead of both shoes pointing straight ahead, when Aunt Gwen hailed him from the bottom of the stairs.

She was standing there patiently holding two baskets: the one covered with a checkered cloth contained freshly baked bread, an apple pie and a pot of quince jelly. The other one was empty apart from a pair of man-size mittens which she passed across to Miles. Then, before he skipped downstairs, she tucked a handful of walnuts into his pocket. 'Make haste,' she beamed. 'There's work to be done!'

Eventually, Miles would gain intimate knowledge of the confusing plan of the ancient port.

There were three main thoroughfares - Beach Street stretched the length of the seafront, Lower Street was the commercial centre with its profusion of shops and businesses while in between them, as its name would suggest, was Middle Street, where 'Noah's Ark' was situated. A profusion of wind cheating streets that smacked of the tang of brine and baccy, tar and tallow, ran from there to the seafront. All carried intriguing names: Market Street, Farrier Street, Griffin Street, Dolphin Street, Golden Street, Silver Street. . .

For the present Miles was perfectly content to follow his Aunt as she strode determinedly along Silver Street in the direction of Deale beach. Here grand houses jostled with modest homes, none of which might remotely be described as 'hovels.'

Built of brick or stone with slate or tiled roofs, they contrasted strongly with the rows of squalid cottages on Miles' family's estate crudely constructed of wattle and daub with roofs of thatch. Miles wondered where rough, rude boatmen might find the money to build such substantial residences?

'Mackerel skies and mares' tails,
Tall ships carry short sails.'

It was indeed a perfect crystal morning. A warm southerly breeze caused a flurry of clouds to scuttle across the cobalt blue sky. Miles was heartened to find that westwards the moon was still reluctant to turn itself into bed. The late autumn sunshine danced provocatively on the gentle waves. It was as if a greedy jeweller had spilled out a bulse of diamonds and was counting his treasure that sparkled before his greedy eyes. Even nature, it seemed, conspired to remind boatmen of the rich rewards to be gained from smuggling, if they were ever tempted to disobey the laws of the land and dabble in the 'Wicked Trade'.

Already the beach was a hive of industry. Women with nut brown faces were washing their clothes in the sea and then laying them out to dry on the pebbles, making it difficult for Miles and his Aunt to pick their way along the shelving shingle. Men with tarry pigtails were sitting on upturned casks mending their nets with large steel needles or varnishing the overlapping planks of their boats. All viewed the pair with suspicion. Gwen chose to ignore their furtive looks, but Miles felt conspicuous in his smart clothes among this tough working environment.

At the corner shop which sold sailor's clothing, or 'slops', a young girl with dark locks was leaning out of a patched on bowed top window and hauling in the washing from a horizontal long pole. Blue trousers, white shirt and red dress. She waved at Miles and he blushed. He tripped over a discarded plank which distracted him from thinking that it was an odd thing for her to have left laundry out to dry overnight.

Beached high and dry were the famed Deale luggers that stood on their own stages among the jumble of capstans, winches and tarred timber huts. These were immense working boats distinguished by their twin masts and square 'lug' sails. They had a cramped cabin or 'cuddy' forward equipped with an iron stove for cooking and bunk beds for sleeping when the crew attempted their longer voyages. Luggers' names were painted in bold flowing letters that expressed patriotism by their proud owners. Miles read them aloud - 'Briton's Pride', 'Guiding Star', 'Young England' - as the pair ducked and dived under their projecting bowsprits which reached right across the rough track that served as a roadway.

There were smaller craft - 'galleys' - scattered among them along the foreshore. These sleek, fast, open vessels were designed to be rowed but as a reserve they carried a dipping lug sail that could speed them through calmer water. Their peculiarity was that they were launched stern first and for that reason they had a distinctive beaching, or 'lute' stern. They were painted white which meant, rather oddly, they would merge with the surf. Charmingly, they bore the names of children, fruit or flowers. On land, they stood out pristine among the rusty anchors, heavy chains and nautical paraphernalia, particularly the straggly lines of greased skids leading to the foreshore.

At intervals, there were galleries and jetties and tall wooden huts with shuttered windows facing the sea. A knot of boatmen dressed in oilskins ('fear-noughts') and sou'westers ('dread-noughts') or knitted blue jerseys and sealskin caps stood on the steps or leaned out of the open top leaf of the doors. They shared telescopes, taking turns to steady the heavy brass instruments on each other's broad shoulders. Their weathered, whiskered faces, scoured with the salt wind, studied the horizon intently. They chewed tobacco or smoked pipes and mumbled comments that were borne away on the light breeze.

'Idle fellows!', declared Miles.

He was surprised by Aunt Gwen's sharp reprimand. 'You would not say that on a stormy night! Their true work involves rescue and salvage which places them in the greatest danger.' She looked over with admiration towards the boatmen. 'They cruise in their boats up and down the Channel for weeks on end, offering to pilot sailing ships whose masters are unfamiliar with these treacherous waters.' She paused and stretched her aching back. 'Sometimes they venture as far as the Isle of Wight.'

The pair strolled down to the water's edge. There was a distinct line of smaller pebbles and a sprinkling of seashells. The waves gently lapped the shore.

'Is the tide going in or out?' Miles enquired, as if posing an intelligent question.

Gwen shook her head. 'Now THAT you can work out for yourself!'

'I suppose,' pondered Miles, 'that if these pebbles were still dry the tide would be coming in... and, because there are bands of wet pebbles it must be going out!'

Gwen nodded her approval at her nephew's reasoning but braced herself for the inevitable further questions.

'And what is that land over there?' He was shielding his eyes from the blinding light of the sun that partly obscured his view of the horizon.

Gwen did not need to look in the direction where he was indicating. 'France.'

Miles expressed his disbelief. This was clearly his first glimpse of the country closest to our own. 'When it's this clear it is generally a sign of bad weather ahead,' Aunt Gwen supplied.

It dawned on Gwen that her nephew would at that moment be thinking of his father. Like all French emigres, he had been invited back to his homeland by the ambitious young military ruler, Napoleon Bonaparte, who was at present enjoying tremendous successes on his campaigns across the Continent. The danger was, of course, that as conscription there had been introduced, Miles' father would be required to remain in France and forced to fight against his adopted country, England.

Wisely, she thought to forestall her nephew. 'Before you ask any more questions here's a task for your sharp eyes. Look out for lumps of coal among the pebbles - there's plenty there - and pop them in your basket.'

'Coal?' Miles tugged on the mittens and wiggled his fingertips. 'Where might that have come from?'

'From a collier brig that sank on the Goodwins last winter. It was rounding the North Foreland yonder.' She indicated the opposite direction to the French coast. 'A squall arose and she sank on the Goodwins, which you can't see at present. Although to be sure it is there, lying in wait beneath the waves, waiting to ensnare unsuspecting sailors.'

Eventually, Miles and Aunt Gwen reached a large patch of clean sand on which were stationed a long row of bathing machines. These curious horse drawn wooden carriages would be run into the sea for shy bathers, such as Miles, himself, to take a dip in privacy.

He paused to look at them. His basket was now half full of coal. The metal handle had started to bite into his mittened hand. 'How much further?', he asked. This time there was no response. His Aunt had wandered further on. . .

They had reached the edge of the Sandhills. This was a wild, remote stretch of land linking the Georgian town of Deale with the medieval port of Sandwich. A winding road, busy with traffic, crossed the sand dunes and sea meadows. This was known locally as the Queen's Highway from the time when Good Queen Bess was carried on a litter in procession between the twin towns. The flat coastline veered easterly towards the Isle of Thanet where there were intriguing caves with dark entrances - perfect, Miles guessed, for storing contraband - picked out at present by the stark sunlight.

Prominent stood the most northerly of Henry VIII's three fortifications, Sandown Castle. This was a squat, round, stone building which, if it could be seen from the air, resembled the Tudor emblem of a rose. Cannons stood forlornly on rotting carriages while sea water had breached the dry moat. It was indeed in a sorry state of repair which was the reason it was not yet garrisoned. Currently, it was being patched up by workmen on the orders of Prime Minister William Pitt in preparation of that anticipated invasion by the French.

Towering over the ancient fortress was a newly built smock windmill. Its boat cap had a fantail which revolved to keep the four skeleton sails or 'sweeps' constantly in the eye of the wind. This would prevent the whole structure toppling in a gale. Despite its exposed location, the mill - like the boatmen

- stood idle because of the lack of wind. All the same, the miller was industrious, preparing for his delivery rounds by loading sacks onto his horse drawn covered wagon.

But it was not the ruined castle nor the stately windmill that had caught Miles' attention.

Between these two contrasting structures of weathered stone or seasoned wood was a circle of trim palings, in the centre of which stood the most enchanting seaside abode that a boy might ever imagine. . .

An upturned boat was perched high and dry on the shingle. It resembled one of the sleek galleys sliced into three. Incongruously, its bow, with a slim door cut into it, stood upright pointing to the sky while the hull and stern had been re-joined to form a novel dwelling.

The timber was silvered larch so that, to Miles, it resembled a gigantic fish that had been thrown up on the beach before it expired. There was the addition of a storm porch, several portholes and a tin chimney protruding from the keel from which smoke navigated its winding way out to sea.

Aunt Gwen nudged open the gate, ingeniously fashioned from a derelict barge's rudder. A cracked cockleshell path wound its way among fisherman's tackle and lobster pots, stacked high against the palings. A drift net was hung out to dry on criss-crossed poles. After a fishing expedition, the bight of the net would have been filled with faintly flicking herring, gorgeous in their splendid livery of silver, purple, green, red and gold, glimpsed only when they are alive or have been dead for a few moments.

There were impressive examples of the sailors' art. An exquisitely carved figurehead in the form of a female goddess stood sentinel beside the porch while nearby a ship's helm was positioned in the centre of a compass, picked out artistically in sorted shades of pebbles.

The occupier had made a brave attempt with a garden, an unusual feature for a home so close to the sea. Naturally, it was past its best so late in the year. Still thriving among the sand and shingle were hardy plants cultivated for medicinal and culinary purposes but there were also banks of wildflowers grown entirely for pleasure. Until early autumn, these would have made a horticultural rainbow with red valerian, purple bugloss, pink mallow, yellow poppy and blue sea holly.

And there beside the porch stood the proud owner looking far more eccentric even than her boathouse. A small woman with a ruddy face under a shapeless hat. She wore a floppy shirt and baggy trousers. She smoked a clay pipe with the bowl upside down - referred to as a 'snout warmer' - as she hobbled around with one cork leg. Miles was both fascinated and repelled by the sight of her but then felt ashamed of himself as she extended a warm welcomed to both of them.

'I've been expecting the pair o' you,' she barked through cracked, yellow teeth.

Miles guessed that their meeting had been accomplished through intuition rather than invitation. 'This must be your neffew.' Perhaps news here already travelled by telegraph? She offered her hand - though first popping her pipe into her apron pocket - as though royalty. Miles caught sight of an antique ring of red gold in which was set a bloodstone carved with a ship in full sail attached to one chubby finger.

'Everyone calls me Queenie,' she sniffed. 'You must do the same.'

Graciously, Queenie accepted Aunt Gwen's food basket before hobbling over to a brazier in which a fire was burning fiercely with an intense blue flame. Miles realised now who the sea coal he'd been gathering was for as he set the heavy basket down. Queenie reached into a bucket and produced a sprat which she snapped in half to show its freshness.

'First o' the season!' she announced before tossing the rest of the small fish whole into a scorching iron pan. 'Caught this mornin'!'

The sprats sizzled and spat while she handed round three chipped china plates which she wiped clean with her apron. She tipped the golden-brown fish out in three equal portions and added a hunk of Aunt Gwen's bread. 'Here y'are youngster. Ger'em 'et!'

Miles settled himself down on an oilskin thrown over a plank stretched across two barrels. Trying to ignore the fish's heads and tails, he tucked into his morning picnic while watching the waves breaking over the distant sandbank, the treacherous Goodwins. The whipped-up foam reminded him of stampeding white horses. The fish were delicious, and he devoured them hungrily. Herring gulls, lured from wintering inland by this brief spell of fine weather, wheeled, dived and screeched overhead.

'And how will you amuse yourself now you're here, my fine young fellow?' Queenie enquired, juggling a mouthful of hot food while balancing her plate on her artificial leg.

'Miles was out late last night looking for smugglers,' supplied Aunt Gwen.

'I wish you luck there, youngster, on a full moon!' Queenie spat out some fish bones.

'And I shall hunt for hides and tunnels,' Miles added breathlessly.

'Now, there you must beware.' Queenie's expression became serious, and she pointed at him with her chunk of half chewed bread. 'Watch out the skeleton don't catch yer!'

Encouraged by his expression of alarm, she decided to elaborate by spinning a cautionary, though farfetched, yarn.

'The last poor fella who went poking his nose about looking for tunnels got himself shut in one and when they finally found him, he was no more than a bag o' bones. If anyone does break into that self-same tunnel, they do say, and I for one believe 'em, that his skeleton comes chasing after them in the dark. The last thing you'd 'ear, mark my words, would be the rattling o' his bones.'

Gwen quickly changed the subject. 'Queenie, dear, we've come to ask a favour.'

'Oh, aye, and what might that be?' She batted the scraps with her tin plate to the gulls who caught them, squabbling, mid-air. 'Ask away.'

Just then an ear-piercing screech sounded from inside the boathouse. Miles wondered if the skeleton had been loosed already and had found his victim deep within the cavern.

Queenie merely laughed. 'Let me introduce you to my mate!'

She disappeared into the boathouse and soon returned with a small, tame parrot. It was an African Grey, a beautiful bird with a silvery grey coat, a white underbelly and a flame red tail. It hopped contentedly from one of her outstretched arms to another before deciding to perch on Queenie's shoulder.

Unchained, the parrot made not the slightest attempt to fly away. 'This is Silver.'

'How d'ye do,' mimicked Silver in a deep, male voice.

Miles was entranced. He wasn't sure whether he dare stroke it. Silver ducked his head under and peered at him, upside down. Miles took this gesture to be an invitation to tickle the bird under its chin. He did so - tentatively - and the parrot responded with a friendly blink.

'Pieces of Eight.'

'Now this bird has travelled the world.' Queenie announced triumphantly. Silver turned his head and listened intently to his mistress. 'Madagascar. . . Malabar. . . Providence. . . Portobello.' Silver bobbed in recognition at each name. 'My 'ubby, lor' rest his soul, brought 'im back from one of his h'escapades in the h'Indian h'Ocean. Silver has been passed from sailor to sailor so you can guess he could spin a few yarns 'imself!'

The parrot ruffled his feathers, lapping up the attention. He stretched his shiny, grey wings and peered at Miles with his beady, yellow eyes. Miles thought he looked very intelligent.

'My 'ubby h'acquired 'im from a sailor who fell h'overboard, poor fella, and he brought him 'ome and now he's 'ere to stay. Cheeky little chappie ain't he?'

Miles was becoming confused and puzzled whether Queenie was referring to the parrot or 'er 'ubby.

'Man overboard.' Silver was now playing to his audience.

'Did your 'ubby teach him to talk, Queenie,' asked Miles.

'Lor' luv yer, no one never taught him a thing! He just listens and copies what he 'ears, more's the pity!' she replied. 'You never know what he might say next!'

'Haven't you something to give him, Miles?' prompted Aunt Gwen.

Miles dipped his hand into his coat pocket and brought out a walnut. Silver danced excitedly on Queenie's shoulder. Miles offered it cautiously, but the parrot took it gently in his beak, then held it in his claw while he cracked it open. 'Them's sharp!' announced Queenie, rather unnecessarily.

'How old is Silver?'

'Who knows? Parrots live for one hundred, maybe two hundred years, perhaps even a thousand. . . or so I'm led to believe. I can't tell whether he's an old'en or a young'en. And if he knows 'imself, he ain't saying!'

'Maybe he came out of the Ark!', ventured Aunt Gwen and they all laughed.

Queenie produced an apple from her apron and cut a slice of it with a paring knife. The parrot pecked at the fruit. After a couple of nibbles, he discarded it over his shoulder.

'Strawberry this Saturday', screeched the parrot. 'Strawberry this Saturday.'

'You'll be lucky!' laughed Queenie. 'Them's well out of season.' She returned the bird to its perch just inside the porch. Silver then amused himself by ripping a torn piece of poster to shreds with his curved beak. Miles noticed one written word before it was destroyed: 'Reward'.

'Care to take a look inside, the pair o' you?'

Miles couldn't wait to respond to this invitation. He fought a path through the narrow porch by kicking aside huge leather sea boots and elbowing past yellow oilskin smocks, both glistening with an accumulation of sprat and herring scales, before popping his head into the darkened interior.

He was keen to explore this topsy turvy world of this unique seaside abode. Queenie had cocooned herself among the most expensive materials - velvet, damasks, brocades - that hung from the low beams and divided up her curious home into separate living quarters. Alas, these sumptuous drapes all stank of stale fish!

Row after row of driftwood shelves, hung high above the the tangle of spun yarn and tarry ropes and discarded sooty kettles and rusty nails, displayed the most exotic treasures - a nautilus shell, a swordfish bill and rare samples of scrimshaw - in the low, arched, cavern. From deep inside a sailor's pine 'ditty' chest she produced a mummified mermaid which intrigued Miles although he was dubious about its authenticity. Each object had their story to tell after they had been brought back as trophies by her late, lamented 'ubby, 'Chippy', a ship's carpenter who had, apparently, 'sailed the Seven Seas'.

Still visible were the hooks for Chippy's hammock that was once strung across the beams.

'Slept there 'anight with his arms folded behind his head to stop him falling out!' Aunt Gwen nodded imperceptibly and Miles maintained a respectful silence. 'A proper sailor, 'e never learned to swim. No point, you see, 'cause if a man fell over the side it would slow 'is ship down to stop and search for 'im.' Queenie shrugged, philosophically. 'If a man died aboard 'is ship, now, they just sewed 'im up in his 'ammock and slung 'im over the side. 'Is ship just sailed on as 'is body slowly sank beneath the waves. . .'

'Is that how. . .?' Miles did not quite know how to form the question as to how exactly Chippy had died. But he was curious to know.

'Tragic, it was, young fella. To think 'e ventured so far at sea only to lose 'is life so close to land.' She let this fact sink in before embellishing her story. "Omeward bound from the Scilly Isles when his barque, 'Venus', struck the Good'ins in a squall. Lost with all 'ands.' She waved seawards where a distinct ribbed line of yellow was becoming visible on the horizon. 'Little wonder they call them there sands the 'Widow Maker'.' Then added chirpily, 'Such is life!'

Queenie ushered her guests outside where they stood beneath the towering figurehead. Miles could see now that it depicted the Goddess of Love rising from a seashell. 'Carved 'er 'imself, 'e did, for the ship 'e was a' sailing in. Said it would remind 'im o' me. Beauty, ain't she?' She tapped it with her pipe bowl. 'Washed ashore along o' his body. That was what comes from going to sea takin' a female aboard.' Miles was forced to admire the comely figurehead while trying not to notice she was baring her fulsome breast, now sprinkled with tobacco.

From inside the porch Silver struck up a croaky chorus of the shanty, 'What shall we do with the drunken sailor?'

'Well, he weren't drunk, that's for sure,' Queenie reprimanded her feathered companion.

Aunt Gwen decided it was time to make their request. 'My sister thought that it would be a good idea for my nephew to have a spell of sea bathing. She considers it will help to drive away his melancholy after his father's. . . absence. There's no doubt he will return,' she added hastily to console Miles, 'in time.'

Queenie produced a handful of brass tokens from her apparently bottomless apron pocket.

'You're welcome to turn up h'any morning early for your dip as long as you've consulted a physician a'forehand for medical h'advice.' She counted out the tokens for the bathing machines and dished them out to Miles. He stowed them carefully in his woollen mitten.

'We'll settle up payment later,' she winked at Gwen. 'Mind 'ow you go.'

The wind was beginning to get up with the turning tide

as Queenie escorted her subjects to the garden gate. All three crunched merrily along the cockleshell path. Queenie, sucking her unlit pipe, waved her guests a fond farewell. As Miles looked back, he wondered whether the incoming tide would lift the boathouse, turn it upright and carry it with its owner far, far out to sea.

Captain Cannons was leading his troops, riding three-a-breast, towards Walmer Castle as Miles ran ahead of Aunt Gwen around the corner of Silver Street. The strong sunshine that earlier had played upon the gentle waves had now moved round to the south and was beaming directly along the length of Middle Street. The Captain raised his gloved hand to shield himself from the blinding noonday sunshine as Miles, swinging two empty baskets, watched in admiration from the narrow pavement.

Captain Cannons commanded the forty-seven Light Dragoons of the 38th Regiment of Foote, newly arrived from Canterbury. He sported the smart modern uniform of a deep blue jacket with white braiding criss-crossed across his chest, red collar and cuffs, a black stock tied around his neck and a stylish white jabeau. He wore white leather pantaloons and knee length black leather boots with spiked steel spurs.

His tall, peaked turban helmet consisted of japanned leather covered with black bearskin and a single red aigrette feather pinned upright on one side. These splashes of red in the uniform indicated that this was a royal regiment. Secured by rings attached to a white leather sash was his new 'Mameluke' sabre whose curved steel hilt glinted in the midday sun.

At that moment, Miles felt his first pang of hero worship - the uniform, the weapon, the mount - without considering that such trappings disguise the true horrors of the battlefield.

While he was musing on a possible future military career an alarming thing happened. A tile that had been dislodged on the roof of the 'Noah's Ark' slithered down and slipped through the broken parapet onto the street below. Miles reacted instinctively. He leapt at the Captain's horse and tugged at its reins. In seconds the loose tile gathered momentum and sliced through the air like a guillotine blade before landing on the cobbles where it smashed into smithereens.

The Captain's horse reared and shied. Fortunately, the dragoon and his mount were both unharmed. Trained to react under pressure, the Captain resumed his composure and settled his sturdy hunter by stroking its trim mane. Then he turned towards his rescuer. 'Boy, you have just saved my life!'

Miles observed that the Captain was a handsome officer. He had a clean-shaven face with high cheekbones, a lantern jaw and ice blue eyes. His short platinum hair was hidden under his tightly curled powdered wig with a brief, square queue.

The Captain, too, was struck by the boy's smart appearance. Most particularly, he was impressed by the quality and cut of his clothes. He seemed totally out of place in the boating quarter of this roguish seaport. But his quick reactions were impressive. This was a friendship to foster. He decided to interrogate the lad and, in a few minutes, had prized out his story.

At Miles declaration of his intention to hunt for smugglers, Aunt Gwen hurried away to supervise the lunches for the customers of the inn.

'We think alike, lad,' approved the Captain. 'If you do discover anything at all suspicious, anything, mind,' he emphasised, 'you must report directly to me. Ask for Captain Cannons at the encampment on the Sandhills.' Abruptly, he took up his reins and signalled to his troops to depart.

'You, young sir, must be my eyes and ears in this infernal town.'

Nothing was said when Miles returned to the 'Noah's Ark'. Silence, though, spoke louder than cross words and the boy was left in no doubt he was in total disgrace. He had not the slightest idea why.

His supper was left on a tray in the far corner of the tap room. It was as cold as his welcome. Just a plate of oysters and a jug of small beer. And, instead of a winter candle to light his way to his bedchamber, he was left to fumble up the winding stairs alone by the dim light of the waning moon.

The day that had begun so cheerfully had ended in abject misery. Aunt Gwen, kindly Aunt Gwen, had reacted frostily to the fact that Miles had befriended a member of the military. It occurred to him that his relatives now considered they had a spy in their camp!

There was worse to come. Uncle Lew had opened a small parcel from his mother which had been concealed in Miles' luggage. It contained banknotes intended for her son's food and lodging. Artfully, she had cut them in half with the intention of sending two batches separately in case they were intercepted by highwaymen. Uncle Lew would have to wait for the arrival of the second halves of the banknotes before he fully gained his money!

Miles felt rejected by his relatives, lonely and confused.

He had to admit that he had even found the interior of the inn completely baffling. The long dark passage ended in a flight of stairs. Most peculiarly they opened up directly into the centre of a wide landing from which led random turnings and irregular rooms. Presumably, these were rented out to guests because their occupants were rarely in evidence. At one end was a shorter flight of stairs behind a narrow door and this gave access via paddle stairs to the attic bedrooms, one of which was allocated to Lew's nephew down from London.

All four walls in Miles' room were built at different angles. There was an impossibly low, slanting ceiling down one side into which was set a tiny dormer window. This gave an intriguing view over the russet rooftops of the old town pierced by the slender spire of a church a short distance beyond. Although situated several storeys above the roadway, when you lay in bed you could hear every whispered conversation from passersby in the street far below.

The room was sparsely furnished: a pine writing desk with a wonky leg, a hard wooden chair with the backrest missing which doubled as a bedside table and a walk-in wardrobe with precious little room to hang clothes. Set along one whitewashed wall - where the occupant would not bang his head on that lethal ceiling - was a slim brass bed.

Miles had been dismayed when he discovered that his lumpy mattress was filled with dried seaweed and the solitary blanket was a boatmen's waxed oilskin. He felt the cold keenly and missed the warmth of his crocheted blankets and the security of his curtained four poster. Every time he bounced onto this bed - or even turned in his sleep - one of the brass bed knobs plopped on the floor! When in his deepest slumber this was sure to wake him up with a start!

Miles had mumbled his 'goodnights' to no one in particular when at last he retired to bed. He slipped the catch and started to undress by the flickering light from the stub of the tallow candle left in the cheap tin save all which he placed carefully on the broken chair. The light was too feeble for him to read so he tumbled reluctantly into his chilly bed.

It was too early to sleep. Instead, Miles listened to the sounds of the old inn settling down for the night. Creaking stairs, rattling windows, slamming doors. Outside, the innsign yawned on its hinges and rocked in the breeze, lulling the rescued animals in the refuge of their floating stalls. Down below, he heard the last of the inn's customers stumble into the street, calling their tipsy farewells and, finally, Uncle Lew securing the bolt at the front door of the ancient inn.

The candle burnt low, guttered and went out. . .

Then he heard a noise that terrified him. A low, groaning sound like an old man breathing his last. Shallow and unearthly. The sound came from inside the bedroom. Yet who on earth could have entered through the locked door? Miles was trembling yet reluctant to reveal his vulnerability by crying out for help. He was determined to control his imagination and apply his mind to fathoming out the mystery.

Sensibly. Logically. Realistically.

Steadying his shaking hand, he reached tentatively for the ring of the tin candle holder. . . slowly. . . quietly. . . carefully. . . This he drew to him and relit the stub by striking a flint from the tinder box. Holding his breath, he raised the candle high over his head. There, at the foot of his bed, snuggled tightly in a fold of the oilcloth and calmly washing behind its ears with a raised paw, was the intrepid intruder.

It was a sleek, black cat.

3

BATHING

A CHANGE in the weather meant only one thing for Miles as he awoke at the crack of dawn, stretched his arms and rubbed his eyes. He trotted over to the window and stared out over the rooftops. The sun reflected his laziness by reluctantly raising its sleepy head above the pillow of clouds. The day was cold; the wind was wild. Perfect conditions for that invigorating early morning dip.

Aunt Gwen had been busy the previous day turning a canvas bag into a pair of drawers - short trunks with a draw-string - that she considered suitable for Miles' bathing. When she held them up for his approval, she saw only his delight in what was actually his dismay. He had shown genuine pleasure, however, when Uncle Lew, in a rare moment of kindness, handed back Miles' locket with its chain that he had pains-takingly repaired.

Miles had dressed hastily without washing under the communal pump. He had a strong idea that salt water would be more effective for cleansing than spring water. Wrapping a towel around his drawers and pocketing his metal token, he made for the stretch of firm sand where the colourful row of half a dozen bathing machines were located.

The Downs Anchorage was a forest of masts. Miles started to count the number of ships riding at anchor, but he soon abandoned the idea. It was an impossible task for there must have been three or four hundred Merchant or Royal Navy ships. In time, he guessed, he would be able to differentiate between all these vessels. He would know, for instance, the difference between a clipper and a cutter, a sloop and a schooner, a barque and a brigantine. And he would be able to recognise the various types of Royal Navy men-o'-war so that he could point out a first from a sixth-rate warship even from the shore.

Northwards, the Goodwins lightvessel lay moored. Recently, it had been positioned there on the orders of Trinity House. It marked the most northerly tip of the treacherous Sands.

It was a robust timber vessel with the single word, 'GOODWINS', painted on both sides of its hull. Three distinctive wicker 'daymarks' were permanently displayed on the triple masts, but these would be substituted by oil lamps hoisted from the deckhouse at sunset.

The purpose of this solitary lightship was to warn troopships of danger when leaving the Port of London and entering the English Channel. Its presence was yet another indication that war with France was imminent. For that reason, its master and crew were already armed with muskets, pikes and pistols. As Miles watched a light, fast cruiser - possibly a frigate - arrived to deliver a pair of four-pounder guns to protect the crew should they happen to be molested by an encroaching enemy vessel.

On the horizon was a strange ship, also moored, and it puzzled Miles. He noticed it lacked masts and sails and was heavily chained, fore and aft. The ship appeared, even from this distance, totally unseaworthy. He wondered what might be its purpose. It looked much like a bedraggled scarecrow, brooding and forbidding.

Miles was dawdling.

Reluctantly, he reached the beach plot where the distinctive red and white striped bathing machines were awaiting the first intrepid morning bathers. These primitive contraptions were wooden huts held high by gigantic wheels with a door at each end that allowed shy bathers, such as Miles, to change in complete privacy. They would be drawn by horses into the water with the tentative bather inside waiting to be attended by a female 'ducker.'

Miles was surprised to find that the same girl with the jet-black hair who had waved at him from the window of the corner slop shop was standing patiently holding the horse in chain traces that would transport his machine down towards the water's edge. This was a tired, depressed workhorse with a conker brown coat, a black mane and limp tail, protected from the bitter weather by heavy oilskins. The girl, by contrast, was bright and cheerful. She wore an embroidered smock and a wide brimmed straw bonnet which half hid her dark, curling locks and rosy complexion. She introduced herself as Jenny as she accepted Miles' payment of his metal bathing token.

Jenny smiled reassuringly at him as she ushered him up the short ladder and through the slim doorway into the cramped interior. There he found a clothes peg, a cracked mirror and a tiny shelf for any valuables. Nervously, Miles bolted the door and began to change into his homespun drawers by the sparse light through the slit windows. He shuddered as the wind whistled through the cracks of the flimsy planks while his feet slipped on the damp sand of the floorboards. The interior stank of rotting carpets. Suddenly, he began to rock and roll violently as the bathing machine trundled down the steeply sloping beach towards the water's edge.

Apart from the indignity of this whole episode, he was convinced that he was about to encounter the most unpleasant experience of his young life.

The previous afternoon, Miles had slipped away from the inn having plucked up courage to consult the eminent physician, Dr Twaddell, concerning his proposed course of healthy sea bathing. He arrived, rather reluctantly, at a grand rented apartment on the first floor of a substantial seafront property, reached via a flight of creaky stairs. Miles tugged on the twisted rope that served as a handrail and when he reached the top step he lingered before knocking on the heavily, panelled door.

'H'enter!'

Miles obeyed this command, and he entered the doctor's study, tentatively. It was packed with dusty tomes from floor to ceiling, strange medical instruments were strewn across a broad oak desk and, ominously, a skeleton for demonstration stared sightlessly from one dark corner of the overcrowded room.

Dr Twaddell was a portly gentleman who, when offering his expert opinion on medical matters, swelled with pride over his own importance so that his ample chest bulged out of his cherry red waistcoat, threatening to pop every single one of its polished brass buttons.

Miles now stood there before him, stripped to the waist, balanced on a high stool in front of the open window of the doctor's oppressive study, facing north.

The doctor walked all round him. He prodded and poked the boy's shivering body with his silver topped cane. Then he looked him straight in the eye through his horn-rimmed spectacles. Then he spoke.

'Avoid all h'excesses.' He took a sip of fine sherry.

'Shun all h'indulgencies.' He took a bite of walnut cake.

'And h'above all, h'avoid strenuous h'excercise' This last piece of advice appeared to be the only one the doctor actually took himself.

Dr Twaddell opened the window and breathed in the salt air. There was such a long pause before he spoke again that Miles began to think that he had forgotten his existence. The bones of the skeleton rattled, and Miles shivered from cold, or perhaps it was fear. A longcase mahogany clock solemnly beat the minutes in time to Miles' thumping heart.

'But since you are not h'actually h'ill, there is no need, in my considered h'opinion, to drink a large h'amount of salt water as they might prescribe in the h'inland spas.'

Miles was grateful at least for that! The window was slammed down shut.

'Instead, a week of sea bathing will h'eliminate all your dis-horders. It is the perfect remedy for every mal-hady. Salt water will dispel your present mel-hancholy.'

Dr Twaddell flourished a silk handkerchief with which he polished his generous, ruby nose.

'Take care, mind,' he rattled his forefinger at his confused patient, displaying a gold signet ring, 'that you h'only bathe in the h'early morning. Wait h'until the weather turns blustery. Do not h'enter the water when it is even remotely warm for that will h'open the pores and you will risk catching your de-ath of co-ld.'

Miles was already beginning to feel a chill as he buttoned his shirt and slipped on his coat.

'That is my h'expert h'opinion. My fee is h'eight guineas. To whom do I h'address my modest bill?'

Dr Twaddell stepped aside as he opened the door for his young client then returned to the window, positively puffed up with pomposity, after offering such h'exceedingly sound h'advice.

Miles had reached the water's edge. There was no mistaking that! Not only did the frantic rocking of the cumbersome machine halt abruptly but a tidal wave of salt water streamed in under the flimsy door facing the sea and swamped the warped floorboards. He could hear the horse being unhitched, turned around in the water and led purposely back up the beach while its mistress, Jenny, offered effusive encouragement.

Thud. Thud.. Thud. . .

Reluctantly, Miles pushed open the door on the seaward side before it was stove in by that persistent thumping. A gust of wind took his breath away. He stood naked apart from his skimpy drawers staring at the relentless motion of the waves that hid most of the wooden steps and half of the iron wheels. He was convinced that he was about to exchange Dr. Twaddell's diagnosed 'slight mel-hancholy' for prescribed 'profound mis-hery'.

'Come along nooow, dearie!' The strident voice gave encouragement. 'Don't be a scaredy cat!'

Miles was helped down the ladder by Deale's formidable bathing attendant, Widow Ducker.

She was a ruddy faced woman with ample cheeks, ample chins and, yes, an ample bosum. She wore a shapeless callico dress that billowed with the waves and a mob cap decorated with frills and ribbons supposed to add a touch of gaiety to the occasion. Her face was pale, her cheeks were pink but her lips were blue. Miles thought she resembled a clown he had once watched performing at a travelling circus and whose painted features and enforced jollity failed to dispel alarm at his energetic antics.

Even Widow Ducker's smile seemed threatening. 'Nuvin' to be a'feared,' she chuckled. 'Trust to the wider,' she beamed. 'Just let yerself gooooo.'

Widow Ducker was a local celebrity. She was in great demand as a 'dipper', particularly with refined folk who travelled far and wide to receive her personal services. Although she did not own these machines, her charges were still expensive - one shilling per session - and, naturally, she expected a sizeable tip for each and every 'dip'. She was a hardy woman who considered she earned her exorbitant fees from working in chilly sea water for hours at a time throughout the extensive winter bathing season.

She was also renown in all the public houses as a raconteur. Invariably, she was surrounded by attentive audiences enthralled by her imaginative reminiscences. She had been present, or so she claimed, when sickly King George III took his first very first dip at Weymouth. 'The King's own baving machine was bootifully carved with the royal coat-uv-arms,' she confided, 'and His Maj'sty was attended by a grand milootary band standing waist deep in the water.' Widow Ducker continued: 'The King's wayward son, the Prince of Vales, has set up in compootition with his farver by baving at the rival resort, Brightoon.'

Miles, by comparison, was small fry. He had been hoping that his machine had been fitted with a modesty hood as they were around the coast at Ramsgate and Margate. Those enormous canvas attachments resembled giant umbrellas that concertinaed down to shield the timid bather from prying glances. He would have been more confident bathing under its dark canopy where no one would notice that he was struggling to keep afloat.

The Widow, known for her 'great tenderness', was about to demonstrate her distinctive style. She grabbed Miles by the shoulders and held him firmly under the freezing waves. Trained to ignore the patient's protests - screams and shrieks - she held him there for a full two minutes. When he surfaced, he was gulping and gasping for air while his arms were thrashing and flailing, wildly.

'Dippy, dippy, go under duckie,' chivvied the amphibious matron, and down he went again.

Then it happened. A freak wave knocked her sideways so that she lost her balance and tripped over the submerged steps. She spun round and round, then was dismayed to find that her charge had been carried far away from her grasp by the strong current.

Miles did not panic. Instead, he succumbed to the deadly comfort of the relentless waves. He was turned over and over in the water like an aquatic acrobat. It was a surprisingly pleasant sensation that lulled his worst fears as he slipped into unconsciousness. He drifted peacefully down for the third and final time to the bottom of the cold, cold sea. . .

Suddenly, Miles was grabbed by his arms and brought to the surface. He coughed and spluttered and stumbled ashore. The Widow's brawny arms, now even more puffed up as if they were covered in barnacles, lifted him up the steps and into the bathing machine where she laid him awkwardly down onto the sandy floor. As he began to regain his senses, he could hear Widow Ducker's frantic attempts at soothing words.

'There, now, duckie, take some deep breffs. You've had a bit of a shock, that's all. Soon be as right as ra-in!'

Miles, in that second, realised he had almost drowned. The memory of this incident would remain with him for the rest of his life. At that precise moment his main concern was that his family should never hear of his horrendous experience. Fortunately, no one, not even Jenny, had witnessed his plight. Forever afterwards, he was ominously silent whenever he was questioned about that first and only early morning dip in the briny.

Miles lingered as he made his way back carrying the soggy bundle of towel and drawers under his arm to the 'Noah's Ark'. He was blue in the face; his cheeks were numb, and he was shivering from head to feet. He needed time to recover his dignity.

He determined that no one would force him to swim for any reason ever again in the open sea. He was in no hurry to return and relate details of his ordeal to his relatives. Hopefully, by the time he arrived, they would be busy with the morning's activities, preparing the inn for its first thirsty customers.

A distant church clock struck nine. Already, Miles noticed five or six carriages lining the foreshore in the vicinity of the luggers and galleys. Coachmen were walking up and down and patting their arms beside their horses in an attempt to keep themselves warm. Ladies were leaning out of their carriages inspecting bales of cloth - brocades, damasks, velvets, silks - held out to them by boatmen. Occasionally just a gloved arm or a feathered cap appeared from within a carriage which signalled either approval or dismissal. The familiarity of the wealthy gentry and the common boatmen seemed remarkable. Whatever might be their association?

Miles walked along beside the conveyances trying to interpret their livery. Several of the coat-of-arms emblazoned on the centre of their doors were vaguely familiar. He stopped abruptly when he recognised one particular heraldic crest - three crowing cockerels - on a stylish maroon and grey post-chaise. It belonged to his mother's former neighbour in Chiswick, the imperious Lady Courtenay, now residing in Canterbury.

This celebrated society hostess had married three times in a relatively short period which vastly increased her wealth and standing in East Kent. She was constantly crowing that she had retained her private carriage when several of her neighbours complained they had been forced to relinquish their own vehicle because of the exorbitant taxes caused by the French wars. Moreover, she was famed for her fabulous masquerade balls. Miles was delighted to think that here, in this remote seaside town, he might renew a former family connection.

Overjoyed, he ran round to the side of the chaise where his head hardly reached above the high back wheel. My Lady, dressed in a burgundy redingcote and plumed hat, was absorbed in examining a length of Lyons lace held out to her by a rugged boatmen. At first she did not notice the interloper. Then, she looked down and stared at him through her quizzing glass. 'Please, ma'am, it's Miles. You are acquainted with my mother, I believe? Lady Harriet from Chiswick Mall,' he stammered.

Miles was dismayed to find that Lady Courtenay's reaction was not one of instant pleasure but abject horror. Her mouth opened wide at the sight of this impertinent young man who had openly presented himself to her. Slowly, recognition dawned.

Swiftly, she disappeared inside her chaise, slammed the door shut, pulled down the blind and tapped on the roof with her stroller. 'Drive on, Yawkins.' The waiting coachman instantly obliged and Her Ladyship's carriage rolled forward on its high four wheels.

The boatmen turned and glared at Miles. His weathered arms were still presenting the scalloped lace. Red faced; he vented his fury on an interfering youngster who had interrupted his lucrative sale. Miles, in a moment of innocence, had made an enemy. For the second time so early in the morning he felt a strong sense of isolation and confusion.

Uncle Lew had been in an uncharacteristic cheerful mood when Miles returned to the 'Noah's Ark'. Artfully, Miles managed to conceal both the traumatic morning episodes. Over a leisurely breakfast he was informed that the second half of his mother's promised banknotes had arrived by the night mail coach from London. There was money to be spent, once the notes were paired. Aunt Gwen advised that it might be used for Miles to acquire more suitable attire for roaming the boatmen's quarter.

This meant a trip to the nearby sailors' slops shop. 'Hubbard's was a tall, corner building with a central door beneath a sweeping bay window that faced three ways: Silver Street or up and down Beach Street. The doorstep was worn down and pitted by the constant passage of boatmen's hobnail boots. Above the doorway, instead of a shop sign, was that long pole with its odd assortment of clothes - green shirt, brown trousers and yellow scarf - which had comically wrapped round themselves by the sea breeze so that they resembled a contortionist at a fairground.

The heavy door was shut fast against the wind. Miles elbowed it open, and a spring bell tinkled. Hanging from the ceiling, folded on the shelves or piled high against a wide central shaft were secondhand, workaday clothes - ticken jackets, kersey breeches, chequered shirts, woollen waistcoats, worsted stockings, knitted caps - for impoverished boatmen and sailors. Staring down at him from a high shelf, where it had made a comfortable bed from discarded clothing, was that mysterious black cat, preening its long whiskers and rubbing its luminous green eyes.

'Don't mind him!' Jenny had been standing by the interior door waiting to serve potential customers. 'He gets everywhere and causes chaos,' she explained, 'but he doesn't bite and rarely scratches.' Miles wasn't so sure. 'You're a good boy really, aren't you, Jinx?' The cat blinked with both eyes which she took to be an affirmative.

Miles explained what he wanted, and Jenny offered her assistance. In no time at all she had completely transformed his appearance with a striped shirt, baggy corduroys and a knitted hat. There was the addition of a woollen greatcoat that would protect him from the bitter coastal north winds.

'A proper sailor!' exclaimed Jenny as she steered him towards a tilted cheval mirror. Miles felt flattered by her comment although he had to admit to himself that his only experience of seamanship was sailing paper boats on the garden pond with his late grandfather.

Jenny appeared to work extremely hard for her keep. She was also versatile. One minute she was serving customers at the inn and the next she was holding the horses at the bathing station. Here she was the assistant in the second-hand clothes shop. She explained: 'My father is a retired boatman. You must have seen him at the inn. This is his shop, but I help out whenever I can. Today is a special occasion and if you care to wait a while longer you will see for yourself.'

How could Miles resist both her intriguing invitation and her disarming smile? She disappeared behind a curtain and returned moments later with two frothing glasses of home brewed ginger beer. Soon loud noises could be heard in the street which directed their attention to the doorway.

At the back of the town there was a multitude of maritime industries. There could be found butchers, bakers, brewers, carpenters, coopers, rope and sail makers. All of these depended on their livelihood from seafarers. And there were several boat builders' yards, the most notable of which was Abel's.

And it was from Abel's the boatbuilders in Middle Street that the commotion emanated. A bevy of burly boatmen were manoeuvring a newly built craft held high on their shoulders around the chamfered corner of a building at the far end of the street. Their boat was a sleek, white galley, twenty feet long, with a lowered mast and eight oars or 'sweeps' stowed inside. Miles noted its name picked out proudly in crimson letters on its bow: 'The Strawberry'.

The men worked as a team so that they hardly struggled to carry their graceful, light craft over the cobbles to the seafront where a small crowd of excited spectators had gathered. They raced laughing with it down the shingle and placed it trium-phantly at the water's edge. Then one of them produced an onion bottle of red wine, bit the cork off with his teeth and poured the whole contents over the galley. It was then turned around and launched - stern first - into the frothy foam by the boatmen who waded out alongside it before jumping in and snatching up the oars. In no time, the Deale's newest galley was half a mile out to sea, its stark white hull merging with the surf.

Hats raised and loud cheers!

It had been an eventful day. Safe and secure, Miles locked himself in his bedroom and flung himself full length on his lumpy bed. And as he bounced on the mattress the loose brass nob plopped on the floor! There was no cause for concern that it would disturb any of the residents because there was still raucous laughter coming from the bar, two floors below.

A letter had arrived from his mother tucked inside the package of banknotes. Now was the perfect time to read it safe from interested yet intrusive questions. She assured him that she was 'coping as best as could be expected' without the aid of his father and that their pet dog, Lucy, was 'perfectly spoiled'. Miles was comforted by the few expressions of affection among the stilted words and phrases. Yet he remained deeply concerned about his father's prolonged absence exploring his inherited war-torn estates in southern France.

After reading his mother's letter by flickering candlelight, Miles was prompted to fold up his discarded clothes and hang them up neatly and carefully, ready for Sunday best. At home, she insisted that he should not leave everything to the servants and had tried to train him to attempt simple tasks for himself.

Half hoping the illusive black cat would venture out of the walk-in wardrobe, he opened it and peered at himself in the mirror hanging on the back of its door. The Miles that stared back at him was not the Miles that he recognised from his London childhood. No longer the haughty son of a gentleman, here was the image of a young working boatmen.

Only his pale hands, face and neck betrayed the fact that he had been brought up in a privileged, sheltered environment. In a blinding flash it dawned on him. Missing from about his neck was the precious locket containing the image of his adored father.

He felt a sudden pang of guilt mixed with acute dismay. How could he have betrayed his family's trust so carelessly! Idly, he picked up the fallen brass nob, turned it over in his hands and consulted the distorted images on its dented surface as though it was a crystal ball.

He had worn the locket that morning when he went to bathe. He had placed it on the shelf as the machine trundled down the beach. It must have slipped his mind as he hurried to change into his warm clothes after his traumatic bathing experience. He was certain he was no longer wearing it when he tried on the sailor's outfit at the corner shop. There was only one thing to do. He must return to the bathing machine in the faint hope of locating it that very night.

Tiptoeing down the main stairs he opened the door and crept along the narrow passage. Customers were drinking, dancing and singing sea shanties to the accompaniment of a concertina.

> 'One Friday morn when we set sail
> and our ship not far from land,
> We there did espy
> a fair pretty maid,
> With a comb and a glass in her hand,
> her hand,
> her hand,
> With a comb and a glass in her hand.'

Then all the customers joined in the refrain by singing, clapping and stomping.

'While the raging seas did roar
And the stormy winds did blow,
And we, jolly sailor boys, were up, up aloft,
And the landlubbers lying down below, below, below,
And the landlubbers lying down below.'

Miles stood on a sturdy settle placed against the wall and reached up high until he could unhook one of the three storm lanterns that lit the long passage at the entrance to the inn. Huddled in his thick coat, he slipped out of the inn. He hurried along Silver Street and, careful to avoid the night watchman who would sing out the hours, turned northwards along the beach. There he located the solid silhouettes of the bathing machines.

They were stationed at the top of the shingle in readiness for the next morning's dip. It was easy. with the aid of his lantern lifted above his head. to locate his hired bathing machine: Number 3.

What he hoped to achieve eluded him. He guessed correctly the doors would be locked. He realised that the machine would have been occupied by later bathers that morning. They would have surely noticed his valuable locket which might have rolled into a dark corner of the sodden floor. There was only the slightest chance they might have picked it up and left it on the little shelf for the owner to find upon his return. How could he possibly spot this through the tiny aperture that served as a window in the bathing machine?

Yet Miles knew that he would not sleep that night unless he had made a determined effort to find his family treasure. He was resolved to try.

Juggling the lantern, he climbed onto the wooden spokes and splayed his feet across the slippery tops of the iron rimmed wheels. One foot on one. . . one. . . just. . . on the other. At least it would not matter that he would spoil his present boat boy's attire. Gaining enough height, he was able to peer through the narrow panel and direct the beam, awkwardly, from the lantern onto the shelf below.

Miles could not believe his eyes. What he glimpsed in those few moments astounded him. The bathing machine was stacked high from floor to ceiling with kegs of spirits. Gin, rum and brandy.

Contraband!

4

TEA

UNOBSERVED, Miles slipped out of the 'Noah's Ark' early the next morning and hurried along the seafront the short distance northwards. He clapped his mittened hands tightly under his arms to keep them warm and pulled his woollen hat down against a sly wind. The sun was yawning over the horizon, its sleepy rays casting their uncertain spell over the rippling waves. An icy mist still hovered drowsily over the undulating expanse of the Sandhills.

A sinister cormorant flew low across the water, its sleek back almost awash, before diving deep for a fish, seeming never to surface. Inland, an acrobatic kestrel hovered menacingly over a possible prey, then changed its mind and thwarted, flew further along the coast. A skulking dog fox, its belly full, burrowed beneath a thicket of sea buckthorn, leaving behind a bloody wreath of feathers, the remnants of an ill-fated, plump goose.

The gigantic Union Jack was being unfurled preparatory to its being hoisted over the crumbling castle where waves lapped lazily against its serpentine walls. The sails of the neighbouring windmill had not yet begun to turn, and the towering structure remained desolate and forlorn. The carthorse was yet in its sturdy stable, feeding from a nosebag before being hitched to the delivery cart in preparation of the morning round.

Alongside the Ancient Highway, which twisted and turned its tortuous way among clumps of black heather and stunted broom towards the neighbouring port of Sandwich, a lone gibbet was silhouetted against the reddening sky. Its iron cage tightly gripped the rotting remains of a hanged malefactor, Captain Coffin, a notorious pirate captured in the Great Downs. His decaying flesh would be attacked by carrion crows when his crumbling bones gradually slipped through the iron bounds. At present, though, it swung to and fro, creaking in the biting breeze, an accusing finger, high above the heads of indifferent travellers. To add to the air of gloom, black headed gulls circled overhead, a grim carnival of executioners still wearing their fearful masks, impatient for an assault on their next terrified victim.

Miles, his warm coat wrapped over his work clothes, stumbled along the beach towards the military encampment that lay but a small mile out of Deale. This was a temporary affair providing emergency shelter until the barracks and the castles were declared fit for habitation. Miserably, it consisted of a tumbledown barn flanked by an assortment of tents, one of which contained stores closely guarded by the bullying Quartermaster. They were ringed by a series of light carriages, carts and wagons relating to the armoury, saddlery, forge and forage departments of the British Army.

The company of dragoons was already stirring. The nimble horses were being led from their stabling ready to be baited and bridled. The brawny cook, after heaving a heavy iron cauldron over an open fire, began stirring the thick gruel that would serve for breakfast, the first of the morning's wholesome rations. A pair of youthful drummers were preparing to rouse the sixty light and active troopers from their uncomfortable night's slumber in the draughty timber shelter. They would be marched informally to the seashore where a chilly dip would revive them ready for their service of long day's active duty.

As Miles approached, he was challenged by an alert sentry but, since he posed little threat, he was allowed to pass and enter the temporary enclosure. Captain Cannons, himself, appeared from inside his personal tent. He was stripped to the waist with his braces hanging loosely over his breeches after just completing his ablutions. He dried his athletic arms and chest before resting the towel across his broad shoulders and surveyed his early morning visitor, inquisitively. Miles thought he resembled a bare-knuckle prize-fighter that his father once took him to watch, competing illegally in a clearing in Epping Forest.

Captain Cannons bestrode a folding camp stool as he listened intently to Miles' breathless account of his discovery of contraband in the bathing machine. He stared at the boy with those penetrating ice blue eyes. Then he made a snap decision and sprang into action. He dressed, armed and mounted his hunter, ordering half a dozen troops to jump smartly to attention and 'saddle up'.

Before he left, he stooped down from his mount to whisper confidentially to Miles. 'You have done well, young sir. You are to be congratulated. Together we will stamp out this Wicked Trade.'

Miles watched in admiration as this handsome officer commanded his men with such authority and assurance. As they rode swiftly across the Sandhills towards the foreshore the Captain's praise was still ringing in his eager ears.

Lady Courtenay was flattered to find that she was attended by an armed escort as she strode along the seafront in the early morning breeze towards her allocated bathing machine: No 3. She was appropriately attired for her early morning bathe. She was wrapped in an expensive woollen mantle, sporting a plaited straw hat with ostrich plume, and her elegant hands were ensconced in a chained fur muff.

The way ahead was restricted by a ring of half a dozen mounted troopers. Her maid followed her at a respectful distance carrying aloft her bulging canvas bag containing bathing requirements. She held the bulky bundle so reverently that she might have been presenting the crown jewels. They were both annoyed - mistress and maid - to find that they were prevented that chill morning from passing further along the beach.

'Find out, Polly, what is going on.'

The maid, who had been eying up one of the dashing young soldiers, willingly obeyed her mistress's imperious command. She was used to being despatched to uncover the latest gossip. She then relayed her unreliable news in the evening while she was dressing her mistress for supper or brushing her hair before she retired to bed. In this unscrupulous manner, Lady Courtenay rapidly acquired the dubious reputation of being Deale's own 'Mistress of Misinformation'.

Polly was prising the details from Jenny who was involved in both calming the horses and comforting Widow Ducker. She was enthralled to hear that the same machine allocated to her mistress was suspected of concealing contraband. . . when there was an almighty crash. The troopers had mounted the steps and smashed down the door to the machine. One glance inside told them that it was. . . empty.

'Check the others!' The Captain's barked order was instantly obeyed. The rest of the dozen or so bathing machines were inspected in the same aggressive manner but they, too, revealed precisely nothing. 'It seems we are too late!'

By now Miles had appeared along the beach, huffing and puffing, but desperate to learn the consequence of his personal intimation to Captain Cannons. He could tell instantly that the outcome had been negative, and his heart sank. For the first time Miles realised that the Captain of Dragoons had a violent temper when he was vexed. He hoped with a sharp intake of breath that this anger would never be directed against him. Clearly, here was a man to be neither challenged nor crossed.

There was, by now, an inquisitive crowd gathered at a safe distance from the row of bathing machines.

Lady Courtenay was relating to Lady Summerson, who had just that minute sauntered past on her sprightly mare, that she thought a French spy was cowering in her very own machine. Lady Summerson rode on but paused to inform Lady Wickford who was about to step into her closed carriage that she had reason to believe French prisoners-of-war had been caught redhanded while attempting to escape. Lady Wickford stopped anyone that cared to listen to her that she had it 'on the very best authority' that an invasion was imminent by the dastardly French.

By now, Lady Courtenay had run out of fresh information to relay. For the moment, at least, there was a marked absence of credible news. She was acutely annoyed that she was no longer the centre of attention. Even her maid had deserted her and was chatting to lowlier servants leaning out of their lower windows further along the seafront. Luckily for her, Sir George Wolfendon walked past, swishing his cane with one hand and clutching his tricorn with the other. As the local Member of Parliament, he was frankly feared by most of the residents who tactfully steered clear of his grand presence whenever he deemed to appear in public. Lady Courtenay, however, did not fall under his spell but instead beckoned him over with one finger from across the pebbly street.

'My Lord, you are used to speaking in public,' she accosted him. 'Pray call my servant, Polly!'

Fortunately, the whispered conversation that ensued between Miles and the Captain went unheard, and therefore could never be repeated, by anyone except themselves. 'You were not wrong, my lad. Contraband has certainly been concealed in one of these clumsy machines. Take heart! We are by no means beaten at our game.' He marched towards his waiting mount. 'Meet me here at two this afternoon. Tell no one.'

And so, at two o'clock precisely Miles was standing in that very same spot when a far larger contingency of Dragoons came galloping along the foreshore and dispersed along the side streets at the North End. Captain Cannons had returned to exact his revenge by tracking down contraband concealed in the houses of the little seaside town. His intention was to explore methodically every one of the winding streets that gave shelter from the biting east winds. It was as if Deale, itself, were a sailing ship cast upon the billowing sea.

This time his systematic house to house rummage would be assisted by Revenue Men and it was certain to reap rich rewards.

In Silver Street a cunningly concealed hide was discovered

after much searching beside the fireplace in the first-floor bedroom of a private house. A trapdoor revealed a rickety wooden ladder that gave access down into a small room beside the chimney stack on the ground floor below. The large quantity of stored silks, velvets and brocades, permanently kept dry by the warm position of their secret compartment, would never have been discovered without first measuring the deliberately confusing dimensions of the two rooms, one immediately above the other.

In Golden Street, which lay parallel, three dozen ladies' kid gloves wrapped in oilskin were found hidden under floorboards of a modest house. Miles surmised that a pair of these charming accessories would be a wonderful present for Jenny who he imagined might one day become a distinctively fine lady.

Along Farrier Street, Miles heard a tremendous commotion. The soldiers had discovered a quantity of tobacco hidden in the cellar of a large, terraced house. The owner appeared angrily at his door as the dozens of sacks in which it was contained were loaded onto a handcart. The incident was about to turn violent when Captain Cannons himself intervened. To avoid punishment, which inevitably meant imprisonment, he ordered the householder to take a wheelbarrow up to the seafront, load it with shingle from the beach and tip the entire contents into his cellar. He was to do this repeatedly until the cellar was full to bursting, thus ensuring that it could never again be used for the purpose of storing contraband.

And while this work was in progress there was another distraction. Granny Penance, who ran a lowly boarding house, stood in her doorway in Market Street. She harangued the soldiers who were making a search of her cramped rooms. She complained that she had been rudely disturbed while taking 'forty winks', after her midday meal. She waved a wooden spoon with which she threatened to beat anyone else who dared to cross her threshold. She was only silenced when her mattress was thrown roughly from the upstairs window. When it landed plump on the cobbles the soldiers ripped it open to reveal packets upon packets upon packets of uncustomed tea!

As the light was fading, Captain Cannons sought out his young companion who he found sitting solitary on the beach. He was in a genial mood now that his diligent examination of the boatmen's properties had proved profitable. But he was realistic enough to know that his men had merely scratched the tip of the iceberg. There was still a vast amount of contraband, to be sure, carefully concealed around this disreputable town.

He was contemplating applying to Prime Minister William Pitt, who, as Lord Warden, was residing presently at Walmer Castle, to apply for reinforcements to be sent down to Deale. They would be necessary in assisting him in his future searches, particularly for elusive underground passages. There was just the pressing problem of billeting soldiers in the bustling town.

'Are you not frightened of the skeleton?' asked Miles when the Captain relayed his intentions to him. 'The one that haunts the smugglers' secret tunnel.'

'That sounds like pure fantasy,' he scorned. 'Stories such as this are intended, I vow, to prevent me from poking my nose in any further!' The Captain laughed. Then he lowered his voice. Once more he took Miles into his confidence. 'What we need are plain hard facts. Inside information such as you have provided is incalculable. You will not go unrewarded for your endeavours. So far you have been of great service to the Crown.'

'King and Country?'

The Captain nodded.

'Often the information we receive is reliable and, indeed, invaluable but we often obtain only half the facts. That is tantalising and makes our work more difficult. It's like fitting together a jigsaw. We need all the pieces to complete the puzzle.'

He shook his head in despair.

'For instance,' he confided, 'we are keeping a close eye on a newly built boat - it's a sleek galley - that we believe will make a return 'run' over from France. Problem is, we don't know exactly when she will be launched.'

He tapped his glove thoughtfully in the palm of his hand.

'Obviously, we cannot conceal troops along three miles of coast to watch night after night without being ourselves observed. In any case, that would give the game away. So, you see, Miles even this tiny bit of information can be frustrating.'

The Captain whistled through his teeth as he surveyed the entire length of the foreshore. It was as though he was trying to conjure up an accurate picture in his mind's eye of the crucial night ahead. Idly, Miles picked up a handful of pebbles and turned them over in his mittened fingers.

'What is the name of the boat, Captain?'

'The Strawberry.'

Miles dragged up from his memory a phrase that he had heard spoken recently. After a lengthy pause he said with quiet confidence, 'I think I already know the answer to your question.'

Now he had the Captain's undivided attention.

'The Strawberry' sails this Saturday.'

'How could you possibly know that my young friend?'

Miles smiled. He chose a smooth pebble, went over to the water's edge and skimmed it expertly across the waves.

'A little bird told me!'

It is often remarked upon that the wealthier residents of Middle Street have the peculiar habit of leaving their curtains and drapes open all evening and, indeed, for the most part of the night. Evidently, this is to allow passers-by the grand opportunity to peer into their windows and to admire their evident fortune and excellent taste.

Miles, returning to the inn as dusk fell, paused to peer through the front window of 'Vane House'. This was a handsome red brick building with fashionable sash windows facing directly onto the street. And it will be remembered that it could readily be distinguished by the wrought iron weathervane and also the ornate carved stone name plaque set into the outside wall.

Further it boasted an open courtyard on one side of the house where, this late afternoon, a familiar maroon and grey post-chaise was parked. The one with the crest of three crowing cockerels.

The boy experienced a pang of homesickness as he tiptoed on the narrow pavement in his borrowed work clothes to stare into the window at street level. Certainly, the interior reflected the occupant's substantial wealth and exquisite taste. The firelight glow revealed a cosy parlour, neat and square, warm and inviting. It was, in a word, 'snug'.

The little room that Miles observed was sparsely furnished yet certainly tasteful. The walls above the pine dado were covered in a soft floral wallpaper while the curtains were of best white dimity. Everything exuded warmth, comfort and, yes, indulgence. It contrasted strongly with Miles' present cramped, cluttered and cobwebbed chamber in the attic of the adjacent ancient inn.

Mrs Croft was the proud occupier of 'Vane House'. She posed beside the fireside in her fashionable gown of cream and plum stripes, an Indian cashmere shawl draped over her shoulders and a dainty lace cap pinned to her generously curled grey wig. In her mind's eye she was the hostess of an exclusive assembly at a London salon. In reality, she was entertaining two minor gentlewomen from the country to afternoon tea in her comfortable seaside home.

Her friend, Miss Lennard, fresh - thirty years ago - from the Canterbury stage had been hired at little expense to entertain the company. In return for lavish compliments, she was most anxious to oblige her hostess. This was, she decided, to be her 'comeback' to the concert halls. She had spent the morning preparing, not by rehearsing, but by dressing the part. She plastered her pock marked face with white lead and dabbed her dimpled cheeks with cochineal. She teased a tired puce silk gown over her stout figure and adorned her bright egg yolk wig with ribbons and feathers. All this warpaint. . . she bore an uncanny resemblance to Hiawatha.

When she surveyed herself in her looking glass, checking that her leather beauty patch was correctly positioned near her upper lip to indicate that she was 'flirtatious', she was fully satisfied that her reflected image presented a yet youthful figure.

Confidently, perhaps too confidently, she decided to abandon her ivory fan which she invariably held against her mouth, not to cool herself, far from it, but to disguise her bad breath and rotten teeth.

The third of these three graces was, as might be guessed, Lady Courtenay. She was staying as an invited guest and needed little encouragement to make herself at home. She had changed into an orange and brown silk gown whose clashing colours, unintentionally, accentuated her waspish personality. Evidently, she had been displaying her recent purchases from the Deale boatmen for there on the sofa beside her were spread out seductively these very bargains: three yards of rose-pink figured silk and four more of turquoise blue taffeta, their crisp, crinkly sheen shimmering in the wall wax lights. The former material would be worked by her seamstress into an evening dress to be worn at ballrooms and supper parties; the latter into a morning gown for leisurely visits or strolls in Hyde Park. She intended to be, at every waking hour, the 'belle of the ball'.

Such was each of these three ladies' demonstration of their own peculiar vanity.

Mrs Croft was married to a sea captain who was at that very moment thumping around in a Royal Navy frigate, 'Tamar', on the North Sea. She was still desperately in love with her husband, although they had been married for a dozen years, and her friends knew - how they knew! - her to be a bundle of nerves every time the adoring couple were parted.

Occasionally, she had inveigled her way aboard his ship, and she had shared his cramped cabin on several short voyages, often boasting that she had never been seasick, 'at least not after the first twenty-four hours'. Captain Croft was ruthlessly ambitious, and he was determined to rise swiftly through the ranks - from Blue to White to Red - until he achieved his avowed intention of being appointed Admiral of the Fleet.

Captain Croft had attained his current rank by patronage rather than talent or endeavour. He had taken part in several naval engagements already where he enjoyed the enviable fate of being forever on the winning side. He had invested his prize money in blue and white porcelain, acquired mainly from fellow officers returning from the Far East, examples of which were displayed on the prized bamboo cabinets dotted around 'Vane House'.

There were further indications of the Captain's maritime associations: a vibrant seascape of a first rater beating down the windswept English Channel (Dover Castle discernible atop the famous White Cliffs) and a pine longcase clock whose painted panels featured a sailor bidding farewell to his sweetheart on either side of the dial with, above, a mechanical sailing ship pitching and plunging rhythmically on tinplate waves.

It displayed excellent craftsmanship and, since it was in full working order, the wealthy owner had obviously paid Mr. Pitt's greatly resented five shillings tax on privately owned clocks.

The clock tinkled four o'clock (local time). This gave the hostess a gentle reminder that tea, which was the sole purpose of her late afternoon's gathering, was due to be served.

She tugged the bellpull by the chimney breast to summon her housemaid then sailed across to the window and opened the top quarter in order to air her neat, stuffy parlour.

Miles ducked down. From now onwards he would have the opportunity to overhear the occupants' affected conversation. He bobbed up.

Mrs Croft turned and brought a tortoiseshell tea caddy from a wall cabinet to the side table. She produced a key from her cleavage and unlocked the box. 'One can never,' she confided, 'trust the servants.' Inside there were two zinc lined containers flanking a glass mixing bowl. One held Bohea, an aromatic green tea, and the other Gunpowder, a pungent black tea named by merchantmen from its resemblance to lead shot. Deftly, she mixed samples of the two with a silver caddy spoon whose bowl was shaped like a scallop shell.

The housemaid duly appeared with a laden tea tray which she set down carefully on the mahogany side table. She curtsied and departed. The focus of the room was now squarely upon the china tea service. This was the latest gift from Captain Croft. He had ordered it directly from the Worcester factory. For Mrs Croft, it was her pride and joy. And now she offered her privileged guests the opportunity to envy her good fortune.

Centrepiece was the small china teapot with its ribbed body and snub spout. It was accompanied, however, by three matching dainty tea bowls ensconced in their deep saucers. The complete service was gilded, and hand painted in a delicate pattern of entwined oak leaves. It was most certainly beautiful. Alas, after fifteen minutes there was nothing more left to admire and so their hostess was reduced to preparing the actual tea.

Mrs Croft lit the spirit burner beneath the silver-plated kettle with a smouldering taper. She had been particular in turning up the lace sleeves of her gown so that her companions might compare the silky-smooth whiteness of her skin with the milky lustre of her newly acquired china. She leaned back in her chair, cupped her hands and gave herself time to absorb the effect her studied elegance might have on her guests.

'I hear they train monkeys to collect tea leaves from the high branches of trees in China,' piped up Miss Lennard.

This comment completely broke the spell.

'Dr. Twaddell warned me he thought it sinful to drink beverages from a heathen country,' announced Lady Courtenay.

This was calculated to make matters worse.

'Mrs Croft always manages to acquire a quantity of cheap tea from our dear boatmen,' confided Miss Lennard. 'They arrange for the East Indiamen to pass crates of it over the side as they enter the Downs.'

'She should examine tea most carefully before she purchases it,' advised Lady Courtenay. 'They have been caught adulterating it with all kinds of things, including sheep droppings!'

The tea party that afternoon was not going quite the way Mrs Croft had intended.

'Miss Lennard, why don't you amuse us with your singing while we await the boiling of the kettle?' prompted Mrs Croft.

Her friend graciously nodded her acquiescence. She positioned herself in an alcove, took up a pose with her silk handkerchief, sighed deeply and began to trill. The two ladies were unprepared for the haunting melody that emanated from this elderly, eccentric entertainer.

'All in the Downs the fleet was moor'd,
The streamers waving in the wind,
When black-ey'd Susan came on board,
'Oh, where shall I my true love find?
Tell me, my jovial sailors, tell me true,
If my sweet William sails among your crew.'

The audience clapped and the singer blushed. Their appreciation was interrupted by the shrill hiss of the pouting kettle. Everyone's attention turned to the ritual of afternoon tea.

Mrs Croft swilled her precious teapot with hot water before popping in three level spoonful's of loose tea, handling the mixture as if it were gold dust. She poured the hot water over the leaves and waited for the infusion to brew.

As a precaution she blew into the spout before the precious tea was poured, floating leaves were removed with a mote spoon and white sugar, fresh chipped from the conical loaf, was offered with exquisite silver nips. And now the moment had arrived for Mrs Croft to hand round the tea bowls, their saucers and spoons to her favoured guests.

The opportunity was not lost to offer them a lecture on the etiquette of tea drinking.

'If you will permit me to say, my dear Lady Courtenay, it is not considered polite to clutch the bowl but to hold it between thumb and third finger with the little finger aloft, like so.'

Lady Courtenay adjusted her grasp of her tea bowl.

'And if I may be so bold, it can never be good manners to touch the side of the bowl with the spoon as this would annoy the sensitivities of the company.'

Lady Courtenay paused in her vigorous stirring.

'And my dear, if I could just point out. . . just in case you do. . . it is also a common mistake to hand back the bowl without the spoon as the hostess will take this as a sign that you would want it replenished. And then you might be awash with a dozen or more cups of tea in succession!' She tittered at her own joke, as weak as her tea.

'Is it permitted in polite company, pray, to take a sip before the tea gets cold?' countered Lady Courtenay. The ladies laughed to hide their embarrassment at this icy barb. They sat contentedly making pictures in the flickering applewood fire.

All this time Miles was peering into the room, his nose pressed against the window glass.

He was contemplating whether the Dragoons had considered searching 'Vane House' as well as the boatmen's homes for untaxed tea, sugar, dress materials or costume accessories. Presumably, because these ladies of quality confined their involvement in smuggling to making purchases they were absolved from admonition.

Suddenly, Lady Courtenay espied Miles' comical appearance pressed against the windowpane. She cried out in alarm but, alas, as she reached for her pistol concealed in her muff lying beside her, she spilled the precious tea all over her dress, the sofa and valuable rugs.

Mrs Croft, stately as a galleon, strode over to the window and pounded on the glass to startle the eavesdropper. She pushed up the upper frame and closed the snob screen, formed of folding shutters, to shield the bottom half of the window from further voyeurs.

'It was nothing more than one of the common boatmen's children,' she assured her guests. 'They have a habit of looking in to observe their superiors. He was probably trying to see what he might steal. That is the trouble with having windows that face directly onto the street.'

'You are lucky to have any windows at all', commented Lady Courtenay, dabbing at her damp purchases. 'Mr Pitt's window tax has forced us to brick up almost half the windows in our mansion. We sit in partial darkness all winter long. It's what I call 'daylight robbery', she bewailed as she handed back her bowl, pointedly clattering the spoon in the swamped saucer.

The shy new moon played hide and seek with the clouds as 'The Strawberry' slipped out of Calais Harbour under the cover of darkness. The mild southerly wind blowing up Channel favoured the new galley for its return trip, but the crew declined to hoist their sail for this risked blowing them irretrievably off course. The eight burly boatmen would rely upon their skill, muscle and, above all, teamwork to row through the boisterous swell of the open sea under that inky black sky.

The contraband aboard 'The Strawberry' on its first audacious 'run' reflected the fact that it was a moderate craft. It consisted of tobacco hidden in a false keel and tea in the hollow mast laid across its thwarts. Small goods of high value. The anonymous boat owner had confidence enough in his hired crew to have taken orders in advance. His local customers would offer cash, but he allowed the London gentry to pay by banker's draft or cheque. After all, the returns were huge and assured. Sale of the illegal goods would bring rich rewards and amply compensate if his galley was subsequently damaged or even lost.

The English Channel was unusually quiet that evening apart from larger sailing vessels making for Folkestone or Dover. The spring tide following the new moon meant that not only was it a time of extreme high and low water but that the tidal flow would run faster, greatly assisting the speed of the gallant rowing boat. The burly crew of the Deale galley made steady progress, travelling in a near diagonal line, for their twenty-two miles bleak sea crossing. After two hours they passed the halfway point. Even then, the boatmen showed no sign of flagging but continued to demonstrate their stamina and seamanship.

It was approaching midnight when a revenue cutter in full sail appeared out of nowhere like one of the famed ghost ships of the Goodwins.

The Collector of Customs, acting on information received of Captain Cannons from an undisclosed source, had commanded the Admiralty's finest cutter to patrol the Kent coast that Saturday night. Its captain, Lieutenant William Dobbins, had been ordered to keep a sharp look-out for a rogue galley making its return trip laden with contraband from Calais to Deale. Consequently, the 'Greyhound' launched from Dover Harbour mid evening with a full complement of crew in order to keep watch over the Dover Strait.

The 'Greyhound' was a true thoroughbred of the sea, built for exceptional speed, strength and firepower. Curiously, the naval cutter had been constructed in the same south coast boatyard as the lugger that she had espied with uncustomed tea on her maiden voyage. She was considered the fastest ship afloat and would soon gain her reputation as the 'scourge of smugglers'.

This superior Royal Navy cutter had an immensely strong hull to support its mass of sails and a broad beam to accommodate its two suspended gigs reserved for boarding a suspect vessel. Its hull was painted sombre black and its bulwarks gaudy red. Its mainmast flew the revenue flag - a union jack and red ensign with a castellated portcullis. Invariably, the 'Greyhound' made a strong impression when sweeping imperiously out of port although its critics complained she was vastly over canvassed.

The midshipman charged with scanning the horizon for signs of the dubious Deale galley happened to focus upon it, viewed as a bobbing speck, eastwards, in the near distance, through his telescope. His alertness was to be commended because the galley's sides, as we know, had been painted white deliberately to merge with the surf. He skipped down to the cabins below the waterline to inform his commander of the approach of 'The Strawberry'.

Lieutenant Dobbin was at that moment enjoying a tumbler of capital gin toddy - above proof, hot, with sugar - in his damp cabin with the master's mate. This had been drawn from a half anker hidden under the table, one that he had conveniently forgotten to return after his recent successful seizure to the Customs House.

Lieutenant Dobbin adjusted the collar of his blue jacket and reached for his bicorn hat, checking his appearance in the foxed mirror nailed to the bulkhead. He armed himself with sword and pistol and marched smartly towards the steps to the gundeck. Instantly, he assumed command - springing catlike into action - confident that his commands would be precisely obeyed by his disciplined crew.

He ordered the retractable bowsprit to be run out the full length so that he could increase its sail by adding a flying jib to the main triangular one. He ordered the double topsail to be unfurled. He ordered the gunports to be opened on the starboard side to allow the eight carronades, or 'smashers', to pierce the high bulwarks ready to be loaded and fired. Then he watched closely as the galley came into sharp vision, seeming to gain speed, aiming to cross his path, making headway despite the spirited waves.

The 'Greyhound' fired a warning shot from the swivel gun at the stem and let fly the forked pennant to declare her intention of pursuit. The revenue cutter was now in full sail and with colours up, crews armed and guns blazing, she bore down on the valiant galley. She was still a good half mile ahead, ploughing through heavy seas, intending to converge on the cutter at an oblique angle.

Curiously, the contrasting vessels were evenly matched. A breath-taking race was about to take place - sail versus oars - as the rivals sped through the open sea at a fair rate of knots. The outcome of this death-defying race would depend less upon fickle fate or fortune than the expertise of the powerful cutter with its trained crew and the daring of the noble galley with its experienced boatmen.

Lieutenant Dobbin observed the skill of the desperate crew. They had timed their crossing perfectly to coincide with the wind and tide that would carry their sturdy craft relentlessly forward through the seething surf. They worked as a team, straining on the oars and leaning into the catch as they powered their galley through the water. Rhythmically, their oars clunked in the rowlocks, then splashed in the foam, then caught the weak moonlight on their return. It was all perfectly choreographed. And he was left in total admiration.

Thud. . . clunk. . . Thud. . . clunk. . . Thud. . . clunk. . .

He watched intently as, less than a quarter of a mile ahead, 'The Strawberry' began to cross the path of the cutter's bow. Astounded, it dawned upon him that she was making straight for the shallow waters of the South Goodwins. This was madness. Her coxswain was an experienced mariner - he was the only one of the crew facing forward - though he sat in the stern seat, held the rudder ropes and steered by the stars. He would know precisely the course he was taking. He would not dare to stray into those treacherous waters upon such an exceptionally low tide. Surely, his intention was not to direct the boatmen towards those fearful quicksand's.

The Lieutenant ordered his men to transfer to the portside and open its gunports. The carronades of the 'Greyhound' proved deadly at point blank range - four hundred yards - but their target, 'The Strawberry', would soon be out of reach. The foolhardy boatmen had the advantage of intimate knowledge of the shoals and inlets of the infamous Sands. They were prepared to take greater risks than their pursuers and venture into an area of water where access had denied them. 'It's like,' spat Lieutenant Dobbins, 'sending a tortoise to catch a hare!'

The Lieutenant's purpose in apprehending the galley was twofold. Not only would he receive a generous percentage of the proceeds from the auction of the seized goods, which would represent one full year's salary, but he would be richly rewarded for capturing skilled boatmen, especially ones with such excellent physique and stamina, for impressment into naval service.

But then he also had a duty to his ship and his crew. He had been placed in charge of the Royal Navy's sleekest ship. He dare not enter territory where there was a risk of grounding. A seasoned officer, he was a leader of men and definitely no coward. His loyal crew would never consider quitting the deck at the first signs of confrontation. He was ambitious but he was also responsible. He faced no alternative. The danger was too great. Suppressing his high regard for the boatmen's bravado, he reluctantly gave orders for his ship to turn sail.

'Go about!'

The coxswain had indeed driven 'The Strawberry' across the flooded southernmost tip of the Goodwins. It was brave, it was foolish, it was exceedingly risky. But that was the character of the local boatmen. Nearing midnight and a low tide the experienced boatmen ran their galley almost aground on the exposed sands. Then the entire crew dived in the water, hauled their laden craft onto their broad shoulders and began to run in their waders the four or five miles across the hardened, rippled shoals. In this way they managed to outwit the tenacious custom vessel.

An alternative route on a high tide might have been to rely on their navigating skills and row in a near direct course across the South Goodwins, taking immense care to avoid protruding masts and submerged wrecks. But in their audacious chosen manner they had swiftly disappeared from the view of the retreating cutter, far beyond the range of her deadly guns. Concealed by a frail moonshine.

It was only when at last they had reached the opposite side of the sandbank that the crew could begin to ease the strain of their frantic rowing. That last part of the eventful voyage involved zigzagging through the myriad ships at anchor - schooners, sloops, hookers, hoys, ketches, bombs, pinks and snows - certain in the knowledge that any further pursuit from the 'The Greyhound' was nigh impossible. At last, they crossed the Downs in safety and made for their final destination where they beached their boat at their allotted station.

Miles stood and watched from the foreshore by the corner shop under the shadow of that long pole - blue trousers, white shirt and red dress - fearful with anxiety. Hidden from sight among the luggers' substantial shadows was Captain Cannons with a large contingency of dragoons, armed with short, barrelled carbines. As the exhausted boatmen stumbled ashore in the early hours of the morning, they dragged their gallant galley from the water and carried it up the shingle, following the line of bonfires that formed a nautical flare path.

It struck them as lapse - there was a marked absence of hand-held lanterns - and this, oddly, indicated a lack of companions to offer them assistance.

But then there had been no prearranged flash in a pan from a flint lock pistol nor a brief signal from a funnel lantern to warn them they were approaching danger.

The quiet was deafening. Just the crackle of burning wood and the spitting of flickering flames.

The boatmen might have guessed, had they kept their wits about them, they were walking into a carefully prepared ambush.

5

PRESS

MAYOR POWELL sat ensconced in his official carved armchair prominently placed in the centre of the north gallery at St. George's Church. He was attended in his civic duty by the town councillors. The Mayor wore a stark black robe, in striking contrast to the scarlet robes habitually worn by the remainder of the Cinque Ports Mayors, while the links of his solid gold chain of office, with a medallion bearing the town's crest, were tied with miniature black bows. This was to denote that Deale was still in mourning - after almost three hundred and fifty years - for neighbouring Sandwich's Mayor, John Drury, who had been killed in a French raid in the middle of the 15th century.

Evidently, the people of Deale had long memories. . .

Before the Mayor the Beadle had reverently placed his silver-gilt mace on its iron rest. This was the symbol of his authority. It was a magnificent affair: its shaft was decorated with thistles and roses while its head was shaped like a crown. The Town Sergeant had been careful to place its top-heavy head to the left towards the altar whereas in council meetings it would be at the Mayor's right hand.

His Worship the Mayor was in a prime position to survey the

assorted assembly - saints and sinners - that had flocked into the charming Queen Anne church that Sunday morning. Boatmen dressed in their Sunday best clothes occupied the topmost west gallery equipped with its own back stairs. This ensured that if they were called away to serve at sea in the middle of a service the resounding of their hobnailed boots would not disturb the congregation from their deep devotions.

Aunt Gwen had insisted that Miles resumed his normal clothes for attendance at church. She ensured they arrived in plenty of time so that they could secure one of the free pews placed discreetly at the back of the church. These were reserved for poor folk who could not afford to pay the expensive pew rent. She was dismayed that her husband, Lew, declined to fork out the required fee, thus placing her in that embarrassing lowly position.

Miles was more used to his allocated seat in the family box at his own parish church, directly under the pulpit, replete with comfy chairs, footstools and cushions plus, in winter, a glowing wood stove. His parents expected to see and be seen by the worshipping population of Chiswick.

The Mayor fumbled in his pocket under his Mayoral robes and finally produced a snuff box in the shape of a miniature shoe. He slid the wooden lid across and took out a pinch which he carefully laid across the snuff groove between the finger and thumb of his right hand. A generous sniff produced a mild sneeze. This appeared to be the signal for divine service to begin. The organ thundered and everyone stood to sing from memory the opening hymn.

Towards the beginning of the service, the clerk, leaning upon the ledge of the lower tier of the triple decker pulpit, began to read aloud the first lesson from the Old Testament. Everyone sat in respectful silence as he announced in a hallowed tone: 'Psalm One Hundred and Fifty-One'. Directly, the pious congregation, perched primly in their high-backed box pews, turned away from him and looked heavenwards towards their Mayor.

'Thou, that sittest in a lofty seat on high,
Why dost thou ignore the plight of thy people?'

The Mayor struggled to rise in his seat. He adjusted his steel spectacles tied round his fluffy white wig, wrapped his black cloak tightly around him and peered like a vulture on a perch over the parapet.

'In arrogance haughty men oppress the poor hotly;
Let them be caught in the snares they have devised.'

The Mayor took up his silver topped staff and pointed it accusingly at several prosperous gentlemen. They sat with bated breath at his impertinence as its tip hovered fleetingly above them before passing over like the Angel of Death.

'For the wicked boast of the desires of their own hearts;
And greedy men seek only gain and evil influence.'

This was now the turn of the town's shopkeepers and businessmen who quivered and quaked as the Mayor's staff rested over their heads.

Next the landlords and customers of Deale's inns - and an ungodly assortment they were truly - who encouraged raucous entertainment on their premises.

'Their mouths are filled with cursing and deceit;
Upon their tongues lie mischief and iniquity.'

Finally, the disciplined, dragoons, sitting respectfully with straight backs, balancing their helmets and prayer books on their knees, who had marched from their military camp in fields on the outskirts of the town, were targeted.

'They wait in ambush upon my devoted people;
In hiding, they seek to oppress the innocent.'

Miles was amazed at the audacity of the Mayor. He had a vantage point from his seat in the back row of the whole church with its packed side galleries. He looked along the rows and studied the faces of the astonished congregation. He registered every conceivable emotion on their characterful faces - guilt, shame, anger, fear, indignation - as the Mayor's accusative glance fell on all and sundry. Only Aunt Gwen, absorbed in consulting her Prayer Book, appeared to take everything in her stride.

There were audible sighs of relief as the Mayor resumed his seat. After several more hymns and prayers, the visibly shocked Vicar of St George's - the Reverend Onesimus, Balthazar, Mordecai, Trophimus, St. Swithin Jones - transferred from the middle tier to the top of the pulpit to preach. Nervously, he fumbled with his cassock for his kerchief and blew his nose vigorously before turning over the hourglass so that its slowly decanting sand would enable him to time correctly his convoluted sermon.

Whatever hellfire and damnation he might deliver that morning, his captive congregation could be sure it would be less of a threat than their eccentric Mayor's silent reprimand.

After this traumatic service, Miles was relieved to regain his freedom. He pushed through the small crowd gathered at the church door to shake hands and exchange pleasantries with the Vicar. He managed to escape the control of Aunt Gwen but instead ran straight into the clutches of Mayor Powell.

'Hold on there, boy. What's the hurry? You and I ought to become acquainted. After all, for a while at least, we are to be neighbours.'

Miles was resigned to the fact that everyone in the town - from the potboy to the magistrate - knew all about him and his affairs.

He did at least have the presence of mind to tip his hat to this worthy gentleman.

The Town Sergeant, already wielding the mace, divested the gold chain and medallion from the Mayor to return safely to the nearby Town Hall.

Mayor Powell offered Miles a curious invitation. 'Take a turn with me in the chapel field, my young fellow.' He had little choice. The Mayor rested his podgy hand on his shoulder and steered him towards the mole humped graveyard.

They ducked under the ancient spreading yew tree beside the south porch where the ground was strewn with bright red berries. A male blackbird continued breakfasting on them, unconcerned by their presence, while his drab spouse investigated breadcrumbs scattered by a considerate parishioner over a tabletop tombstone.

The chapel field itself was unkempt. Dog roses burrowed amongst thickets which would have been a haven for birds, bees and butterflies in summer. Here, row upon row of tombstones leaned this way and that, like sailors maintaining their balance on the top deck of a storm-tossed galleon.

It soon materialised that the Mayor had a macabre fascination with reading tombstones. He used his staff to part the pervading weeds and then pointed with it to old and new inscriptions: 'Read them aloud. Don't be shy. Tell me what they say.'

Miles had little choice but to obey his imperious command. Many of the carvings had already been obliterated by patches of moss, spots of lichen and swags of ivy. Yet he managed to fill in the gaps by tracing his finger around the florid letters, deeply incised by the skilful stonemason's hand.

'In this vault'. . . *'under a stone'*. . . *'lies the remains'*. . . *'also of'*. . . *"departed this life'*. . .

'Yes, yes, sing them out!' Miles had the strong impression that Mayor Powell knew every word by heart but took pleasure in hearing anew those mournful phrases. They moved slowly and reverently among the bleak lozenge shapes. Magpies chattered in the bare branches overhead. Squirrels hopped along the crumbling boundary walls.

Miles began to appreciate the superior carvings with their primitive religious or physical depictions. Sightless skulls, crossed bones, open books, hour glasses, winged angels and sealed coffins. All were picked out in relief by the wintry sun. There was one poignant image of a skeleton arising from a grave summoned by an angel appearing through the clouds to blow the last trumpet. This, thought Miles, was the stuff of nightmares.

Here seamen found their hard-won rest after serving - for periods long or brief - in the Royal or Merchant Navies as pilots, pursers, surgeons, gunners, carpenters and captains. Several young midshipmen had died from fighting or fever in remote regions during Britain's interminable wars of exploration or expansion.

The unlikely couple kicked their way through the dry leaves - copper and gold - that crackled and crunched underfoot. A gust of wind stirred them, and they spiralled playfully ahead along the gravel path. It was as if they invited playful chase.

Miles paused when he came to one puzzling inscription which ended abruptly:

'Mary of the other side.'

Whatever could this mean? Had Mary passed over to the spiritual realm or had she emigrated to the New World? 'Read what's on the back boy!' laughed the Mayor. And then it dawned on Miles that this particular tombstone was so crowded with inscriptions that the remainder of the epitaph was continued on the reverse!

As they leisurely toured the churchyard, Mayor Powell steered Miles away from the far north wall. There his sharp eyes had observed two or three rotting wooden crosses protruding like tilting masts from sunken vessels among the sea of grass. Miles expressed his curiosity regarding their origin but in return only received the offhand word: 'Heathens!' This was accompanied by a dismissive wave of His Worship's staff before they passed by firmly on the other side.

Finally, they were both drawn to a recent tombstone placed bolt upright in a tranquil corner. 'Look and learn.' The Mayor removed his tricorn and bowed his head. Miles read the pristine inscription with confidence:

'In memory of John Elbeck, a private in the Westmoreland militia, aged 27 years, who was shot in Beach Street, the 26th September 1794, by a person unknown in the execution of his duty while assisting the officers of the Customs. R.I.P.'

Mayor Powell shook his head. 'Someone must know the culprit. Indeed, they must. Despite offering a huge reward the town stays silent.' Solemnly, he replaced his hat.

'Westmoreland seems such a long way away!' observed Miles. 'It is odd that they would recruit soldiers from such a distant county?' Then he thought deeply. 'Is it because they could not trust anyone recruited locally to prise out smugglers, I wonder?'

Mayor Powell had turned his back and had started to walk purposely along a side path made up of discarded fragments of ancient tombstones. Inadvertently, Miles had stumbled upon the truth, but Mayor Powell was not willing to confirm or deny. Nevertheless, the boy's questions continued at a rapid pace.

'Please, Mr Mayor, what is meant by R.I.P.' Miles had noticed these abbreviations after almost every name inscribed on the tombstones.

'It means, my boy, 'Rest in Peace'.'

'And, please, do the dead always rest in peace?' Miles ventured. It was the sort of blunt question that adults invariably shy away from answering honestly.

'That, boy, poses a problem. We hope they do. . . and for all eternity.' The Mayor gently shook his head. After a short pause he decided to elaborate. 'It's not always the case.'

By now the pair were sauntering along by the boundary wall of the church field. The Mayor once more raised his staff and pointed to the Vicarage. 'Often I've sat late at night for a sup of ale with the Vicar in his study. Our conversations have at times been disturbed by an unearthly sound.' Miles showed sudden interest. 'The Vicarage, you see, was built partly on consecrated ground and perhaps it never should have been.

'A vault - abandoned now for many a year - can still be entered by an iron ring set into the chancel floor. It runs from the crypt below, underlies the field northwards and extends. . . yonder. . . beneath the Vicarage.' The Mayor traced the underground path of the vault with his staff. 'When the lower town floods, the vault fills with water and the lead coffins are lifted from their stone shelves. They drift around of their own accord for the occupants, you can imagine, are now reduced to skeletons and the dead cannot steer. You can hear them afloat, thudding one against another, jostling aimlessly for position in the watery darkness. 'It's an eerie sound. . . an eerie sound to be sure.'

Miles shivered. The idea both thrilled and terrified him. He was reminded of the skeleton that dwelt in the elusive smugglers' tunnel that would be resurrected whenever intruders disturbed him from his eternal rest.

As they turned and walked through the heavy iron gates, gentlefolk who had lingered at the church to converse with the Vicar moved politely to one side and bowed or curtsied respectfully to Deale's formidable Mayor.

It was unfortunate for the coachman, Goggins, that Mayor Powell was standing on the pavement outside the Town Hall when the leading horses of his post coach took the corner rather too sharply. One wheel had clipped the kerb of the newly laid paving stones, the introduction of which His Worship claimed sole credit and was inordinately proud. Luckily, there were no occupants of the vehicle for the repaired shutters were firmly pulled down over the draughty window on this bright forenoon.

The Mayor had called by the Town Hall to divest himself of his official robes and tricorn hat and change into his ordinary day clothes in order to patrol the town. Miles wondered whether the band inside the beaver hat he was now wearing would bear the official stamp to confirm he had paid the tax on such an expensive item.

Mayor Powell, however, was deeply contemplating his avowed intention to keep the Sabbath sacred throughout this disreputable seaside town. Inadvertently, Goggins had played straight into his Worshipful's outstretched hands.

'Mr Mayor!' cried the flustered Mr Goggins.

'Bless me!' returned the apoplectic dignitary.

Goggins, renowned throughout the county for his unblemished career, had just now careered into the very person responsible for granting his annual coachman's licence.

'Where, pray, might you be bound?'

Goggins touched the fresh sprig of rosemary in his lapel. He had just been enjoying a sly swig of cherry brandy with his young female admirer, Nancy. The amorous girl was a serving wench at 'The Three Mariners' coffee shop, south along the seafront. She had sat on his knee, toyed with his ear and whispered a favour. Just a teeny-weeny one. Please, please would her dear, sweet, darling Goggonsy-wogginsy deliver a couple of parcels to her brother, Edward, who was staying at the 'Bell Hotel' in Sandwich. He would then take them with him when he returned by the overnight mail coach to his business in the City of London. It contained patterns for a fashionable gown that she could not possibly live without. And to be sure, this was a special favour which she 'never, ever would or should or could forget'.

'I am going, Mr. Mayor, to Canterbury,' blustered Goggins, sweat pouring off his brow, 'to visit my elderly aunt who is not likely to last until the night.' He touched his hat and added purely for conviction, 'Lor' bless her!'

But the wily Mayor was not at all convinced by this cock and bull story. He did not wish, however, to discredit a man the whole town regarded highly. He was unwilling, therefore, to enter into any dispute. Today, of all days.

'Mr Goggins, you will turn this coach about and leave the pastoral visit to your elderly aunt until the morrow. Hopefully, the good woman will survive until dawn.' Sarcastically, he added, 'God willing!'

Goggins was relieved that the moralistic Mayor was not about to take his lapse any further. He adjusted the reins so that his coach revolved slowly until it faced the opposite direction from whence it came. He was proud of this achievement. Hopefully, the Mayor would regain confidence in his superior driving skills.

'Unless you are about the King's business,' called out the Mayor as his parting shot, 'you will decline any further commissions of this kind upon the Sabbath.'

Dusting down his coat and retrieving his hat, Mayor Powell proceeded to patrol the three main thoroughfares. Miles, who had waited patiently by the church gates for his illustrious companion, was summoned across the street to accompany him on his self-imposed crusade to suppress vice and immorality in the town of Deale.

Zigzagging along each of the winding streets the Mayor pounced upon several business that had, in his virtuous mind, flouted one of the ten express biblical commandments: '. . .to keep the Sabbath Day holy.'

In Lower Street, he paused purposely at a half open door under the striped red and white pole of a barber-surgeon. Through the narrow gap he espied a middle-aged gentleman leaning back in a raised chair with his face covered in soapy foam reflected in a mirror. Standing over him with a poised cutthroat razor was the barber who was about to shave his stubbly chin. The Mayor's loud thud with his staff alarmed him so much that his steady hand slipped and nearly cut his customer's frothy throat.

'Have a care there, Mr Barber. That beard will not harm for another day. Both you and your customer are required in church on a Sunday.'

And, with that, the Mayor slammed the barber-surgeon's shop door firmly SHUT!

Moving on, the pair strolled along Middle Street. Here, by reputation, every third house was either a public house or a brothel. Most had complied with the law by closing their doors on a Sunday. Alas, the landlord of the 'Jolly Sailor' had conveniently forgotten what day of the week it was. Noise was spilling out of its open doors. Inside the scene was indeed one of revelry. It contrasted with its dreary exterior paintwork, blue grey, applied garishly from surplus cans surreptitiously acquired from the nearby Navy Yard.

Underneath the colourful sign of a jovial sailor in blue jacket and striped trousers leaning against a large barrel sipping a pint and smoking a pipe, were two weathered boatmen imitating this relaxed style. Pipes in mouth, tankards in hand, they were putting the world to rights when around the corner marched Miles and the Mayor. Without a bye-nor-leave, he took the tankards from them and stormed into the pub and over to the bar. 'Landlord, it has slipped your mind that today is the Lord's Day. Sundays are appointed for reflection and devotion not carousing nor imbibing.' And with this he tipped the tipple onto the floor.

'Cease your jollity, I command you, before I send for the Constable!'

On the corner of Market Street, Miles and the Mayor encountered Granny Penance. She was reaching high with her cloth to clean the narrow windows of her lodging house. When the Mayor accosted her, it gave her such a fright she wobbled alarmingly on her three-legged stool.

'Sign of a guilty conscience!' pronounced the Mayor. 'Can't they wait til the morrow, my good woman?' The Mayor sniffed the air suspiciously, tipped his hat politely and walked on leaving Miles to ponder how come there was such a surfeit of gin in the town that an elderly woman might employ it for cleaning her windows!

On now to Beach Street where a team of boatmen were loading their single masted galley punt with provisions to ferry out to becalmed sailing ships, at anchor. They were so involved in their task that they did not, at first, notice the approach of the Mayor and his reluctant lackey.

'Gentlemen, good day.'

His bulky shadow fell upon the ribbed planks of their boat. The men stopped and turned, making it obvious by their scowls that his presence was far from welcome. The Mayor enquired upon the necessity for their industry on the Sabbath and was unimpressed by their response that fresh fruit, vegetables and, particularly, water were required whatever the day of the week. This answer might seem perfectly reasonable but to the Mayor, unused to be challenged in his elevated position, this amounted to impertinence.

'Gentlemen, desist!' Unwisely, the Mayor, to demonstrate his power, struck a cabbage with his staff. It tipped over the side of the boat and rolled around on the pebbles like a guillotined head. This trivial incident inflamed the boatmen. One of them, assuming command, decided to square up to His Worship.

'And what is your authority for such infernal interference?' The burly boatman struck out his chest and crossed his arms in open defiance.

Mayor Powell was not to be intimidated. He thrust his face full into the boatman's own and tapped him on the shoulder with his staff. 'You sir, mind your manners, when addressing the Chief Magistrate.'

'Go to the Devil and bed----d!'

'You are liable to be punished for this profanity. Be silent this instance or I will place you in the stocks!'

A small crowd began to gather on the foreshore alerted by the affray. Dressed in their Sunday best clothes, they kept a respectable distance. One of them, a presentable gentleman, stepped forward and ventured over to the boat. He was a sprightly fellow despite having a slight limp. Bravely, he had decided to intervene.

'Now, Tommy, lad. Take care what you say. The vegetables will surely keep. We do not want to sour our relations with Mr Mayor.'

The newcomer stood between the sparring partners. The calm resonance of his voice had the desired effect. Little more was said. He handed back the bruised cabbage. The surly boatman turned his back on the Mayor and strode across the beach in the direction of the North End.

Disgruntled, the rest of the boatmen threw a tarpaulin over their produce and heaved their boat up the beach. Anyone might guess, though, they meant to return once the hubbub had died down. Miles decided it was high time he made himself scarce.

Mayor Powell was satisfied his mission for that day was accomplished. Thanks to the intervention of the courageous gentleman his dignity remained unsullied. He could congratulate himself that on this particular Sunday the streets for the main had fallen silent. He had scored a victory in the first round of his sworn intention of reforming the manners of the town's inhabitants. Tomorrow, he resolved, he would order strict new rules and regulations for trading on the Sabbath to be announced by the Town Crier.

Problems resolved, at least temporarily, the Mayor waddled down Silver Street to his grand residence where his Sunday lunch of roast goose awaited. Idle spectators, too, wandered off in different directions to the comfort of their own homes. The boatmen, muttering and mumbling, also dispersed. Everyone conceded it was no good fighting a losing battle.

Inadvertently, the Mayor, unbeknown to him, had rescued these boatmen from an impending fate which would have adversely affected their destinies!

At the upstairs window of the slop shop, Jenny was swinging a small gold chain that sparkled in the last of the morning sunlight. Miles waved to her and she beckoned him. She skipped downstairs and opened the door a margin to let him squeeze through. They edged past the piles of second-hand clothes and climbed the helter skelter staircase, built around a central shaft, to reach the private parlour above the shop.

Miles was impressed by the charming little room with its

fascinating sea view through the huge bay window. The walls were bare matchboard and the curtains plain dimity. Yet each item of furniture - tables, chairs, stools - was constructed of fashionable reed or bamboo. Every surface was covered with work boxes, hand mirrors and picture frames decorated with delicate seashells - cockles, limpets, mussels, periwinkles - in pastel shades of pink, blue, cream and yellow. Displayed on rustic shelves were onion shaped wine bottles, carved nautilus shells and even a tantalising ship sailing inside a bottle.

There were scatterings of Roman coins with indiscernible heads, chunks of amber the colour of old ale and even a delicate purse fashioned from clasped oyster shells. . . all gleaned from the beach. Decorating the walls of the intriguing parlour were cheap engravings of maritime scenes.

A fire crackled in the duck's nest iron grate while in the centre of the mantlepiece stood an impressive brass timepiece. On a side table was placed a creamware transfer print jug of a jack tar bidding farewell to his current sweetheart. A humorous rhyme accompanied this jovial scene:

'A sailor's life is a pleasant life,
He freely roams from shore to shore;
In every port he finds a wife,
What can a sailor wish more?'

Miles was surprised to find that Jenny, a tomboy, was also an accomplished homemaker.

This inviting little room which she kept for her widowed father and herself exuded warmth and comfort. It also perfectly expressed her own ingenuity and creativity.

Displayed randomly on a large pine sea chest were further curiosities - decorated pipe bowls, rusty iron keys, glass phials, pottery shards, chips of blue and white china unearthed in the Sandhills. But the one object that caught Miles' attention lay on a polished table by the window next to a spyglass in a tooled leather case.

It was his gold locket!

Miles stared in disbelief. It had been found, explained Jenny, at low tide when she had been beach combing. It must have fallen through the floorboards of the bathing machine and ended up alongside one of the greased skids. Perhaps this occurred when the soldiers invaded the contraption? She had noticed it glistening amongst the wet pebbles and damp sand.

All this time, perhaps, Miles should also have noticed that Jenny, still standing in the centre of the room, was wearing a delicate printed dress. It was chocolate coloured calico with a trailing floral pattern. 'You look very sweet, Jenny,' Miles offered awkwardly. True, her dress was extremely pretty but, feigning to dismiss her new friend's complement. Jenny simply remarked offhand that it 'went through the winter'. She did, though, give him a bob and a twirl.

Now it was Miles' turn to turn around as Jenny fastened the precious locket once more around his neck. He blushed with embarrassment at this unexpected intimacy. His nape tingled not with the cold of the metal but at the thrill of this first display of affection from an attractive young lady. He spluttered a few awkward words of thanks.

His embarrassment was saved by Jinx who had appeared from nowhere to toy with the reflection of the gold locket as it danced around the room in the late sunlight.

This seemed the moment for Jenny to ask a favour in return. She had decided that she would like to work for Mr. Oakley, owner of Sandown windmill. Maybe she could look after his horses, or sweep the stores, or deliver the sacks of flour. . . and she wanted to inform him of her availability by letter. There was only one problem. Jenny could not write.

In advance of her request, Jenny laid out on the table a feathered quill, a pot of ink and a single sheaf of writing paper. Miles sat down and picked up the quill while Jenny looked expectantly over his shoulder. 'Tell me what it is you want to say. . .'

'Dear Mr Oakley,' Jenny's proposed letter began promisingly enough. 'If you please...' Then came a long pause before she rattled off her dictation.

'IthascomeintomymindthatIwouldlikeverymuchtooffermy servicesassomeoneexperiencedwithhorses. . .'

She stopped for breath. Miles started to laugh. He had only just dipped the nib in the inkwell.

'Speak slowly so that I have time to form the characters. Say what you have in mind and leave me to compose the letter for you. I promise it will be to your infinite satisfaction, my fine lady.'

Jenny sighed, 'There, now, you have broken my dream.'

And, as he wrote, she confided her aspirations to become a gentlewoman. 'Lady Jennifer Hubbard at your service, sir,' she curtseyed, but not too deeply, 'an heiress worth £10,000 a year!'

Miles, who never lacked imagination, was amazed by the reasons for this desired elevation in society from a mere shopkeeper's daughter. He assumed, being himself a privileged child, that Jenny would want a grand mansion in which to entertain her friends, to become a notable hostess offering tea to her friends, ride her own palfrey and own an extensive wardrobe of exquisite clothes so that she would be the envy of the London salons.

Instead, Jenny revealed in a low, steady voice, that to secure a position in society would enable her to assist the boatmen when circumstances became intolerable for them and they were threatened with the parish workhouse. She would open a school for their children to give them an education instead of aimlessly roaming the streets. She would have the means to support her own father financially with his struggling business.

Miles stared at his friend. He was greatly touched by her charitable concerns. As she spoke, she was transformed before his very eyes into that very gentlewoman, exuding elegance and eloquence. She stepped down from her carriage drawn by bays and mounted the stone steps of her country residence. She curtsied to the row of fine gentlemen as she danced before them in the vast candlelit ballroom. Her eyes sparkled and her lips smiled. She looked, in that moment, every inch a fine lady.

He whistled in admiration.

Instantly, Jenny halted him from his reverie. 'Miles, you must stop that at once! You'll bring us all bad luck. You'll be whistling up a wind.'

Realising that perhaps she had been too hard on him she quickly changed the mood to one of practicality. 'Anyway, who would consider marrying the daughter of a shopkeeper?'

For a time, Miles could think of nothing to say. Then he reminded her that he had, in fact, never met her father.

But you have several times. You've just not recognised him. There he is now.' She pointed through the window beyond the empty pole at the polite gentleman who had bravely intervened between the Mayor and the boatmen. 'There is my father.'

'The man who is limping?'

'Yes, that's him!' said Jenny. He injured his leg when he was a boy trying to catch a colt that had bolted from its stable in a thunderstorm.'

As the midday sun moved slowly round to the west, the front of the shop turned to shadow. At the same time the wind began to rattle the glass panes and even lifted the oriental rug. Jenny shivered visibly as she made her way closer to look out of the bay window at the sea. She watched as a 'catspaw' began to ruffle the waves. Then she gasped at what happened next.

Her father had wandered down the beach to inspect a large packing case that had been thrown up on shore earlier that day. It had clearly been ignored by the group of boatmen which was most strange. Normally, they were on the alert for flotsam or jetsam that might be sold at a great profit. He struggled down the beach to investigate.

He took off his shoes and rolled up his trouser legs before venturing in the shallow water.

He reached out and lifted the lid that had been previously prized open. To his surprise he found that sodden case contained stacks of china potties! They would hardly reap rich rewards when offered in the marketplace. Customers would be in hysterics, he surmised, and laughed aloud at this ludicrous idea! 'Curiosity killed the cat!' he thought.

While his focus of attention was upon the washed-up chamber pots, Jenny's father failed to notice a small boat land alongside him on the incoming tide. It was too late for this brave man to react or even flee when he found himself surrounded by a ruffian gang wielding hangers and cudgels.

Helpless to defend himself, he was bullied and badgered to return to the top of the beach where he was confronted by the uniformed Recruiting Officer, Captain Gabriel Bray, who had ordered this general press on behalf of the Royal Navy.

The darker the night, the dirtier the weather, press gangs roamed sea and shore ready to pounce upon lonely, unsuspecting, fit and able men. Merchantmen returning from long journeys were obvious targets and floating press gangs regularly boarded these ships to forcibly recruit trained crewmen. Calm weather had prevented sailing ships from entering the Downs for the best part of a month and therefore the land became a fairer game for the pressmen. Normally, they targeted inns and taverns deep within the town but because Mayor Powell had efficiently closed these premises on this particular Sunday morning they had concentrated on the foreshore.

When warned of an imminent 'sweep' the Deale boatmen also organised themselves into gangs ready to repel the pressmen violently by pelting them with sharp pebbles from the beach. Again, it was the action of Mayor Powell who had insisted the boatmen return to their homes so there was no one on hand to drive them back and into their rowing boat.

Captain Bray took command of Jenny's father and informed him abruptly that he was bound to accept the King's shilling in return for his enforced enlistment in the Royal Navy. He would receive a further three farthings as a reward for good behaviour if he offered no resistance and accompanied them to the mustering centre.

Jenny rushed downstairs and out of the corner shop crying aloud with Miles following hard upon her heels. They both watched helplessly as the reluctant recruit was marched away, still minus his shoes and stockings, under armed escort to the official rendezvous at the King's Navy Yard.

Left alone in the parlour, Jinx jumped onto the polished table by the window and toyed with the feathered quill. The mischievous cat knocked over the ink well and padded through the spillage, leaving inky paw prints all over Jenny's immaculate letter of application to Master Oakley, proprietor of Sandown Mill.

Early that evening the wind whistled down the chimney of the taproom at the 'Noah's Ark'.

A thick cloud of smoke descended and filled the entire room. Everyone started coughing and spluttering as it went everywhere but up the chimney. The blazing log fire shuddered, died down, then rekindled with vigour. This trivial incident had an instant effect on the group of residents who sprang fervently into life.

Everyone recognised that the billowing smoke signalled a change in the wind direction. Flags, pennants, streamers and weathervanes relayed this vital information throughout the town and port. The wind had turned to the north-east. Perfect sailing conditions. Miles, perched on a stool by the fire with a bowl of steaming beef broth, witnessed a rapid transformation of the ancient inn.

Refined ladies and gentlemen betrayed a primeval instinct for self-survival. They perfectly interpreted the warning signs of the weather outside as the candles flickered in their copper sconces and the heavy pendulum of the tavern clock swayed violently. They rushed upstairs to their rooms to grab their half-packed boxes, cases and trunks to take on their long-anticipated sea voyage. Lew Bristowe positioned himself at the top of the stairs to ensure no one passed him without first settling their exorbitant bill. Miles stood in consternation, his supper abandoned along with their wine and baccy on the tables, as the taproom was cheated of all its customers.

Overhead, he heard a mighty clamour - slamming of doors, snapping of lids, stamping of feet and sliding of luggage down the rickety stairs - that accompanied this frenzy of activity. In the crowded passage, pine chests and wicker baskets were lifted, pulled, tugged and shoved by their impatient owners who were tripping and tumbling, bumping and bruising in the stampede to be first to reach the windswept foreshore.

On the beach the entire seafaring community had been mobilised. A fleet of sturdy boats - galleys, punts and galley punts - were lined up at the water's edge. Here was a well-rehearsed routine for the boatmen who plied for the trade of hundreds of prospective passengers that spilled out from the seafront hotels and inns. There was cursing and crying, sweating and swearing, bickering and bartering. Frantic passengers offered double, treble, even quadruple the normal fare to secure the services of the boatmen to ferry them out to their sailing ships preparing to depart from the Downs.

Miles, who had offered to carry a snappy puppy in a canvas bag for one breathless, portly female, was dismayed to find that she neglected to offer either thanks nor praise as she stumbled down the shelving beach. The boatmen had lit bonfires to indicate a safe path through their sheds, tackle and skids to their waiting boats at the water's edge. They held lanterns, torches and flares to guide their passengers across the slippery shingle. These flickering lights held close to their rugged faces made the boatmen look grotesque and conjured up visions of gargoyles dancing devilishly atop church towers. But there were moments of humour, too, when strong boatmen lifted refined women on their shoulders as they waded into the water and heaved elderly gentlemen over the side of their boats prior to launching.

The north-easterly blew smartly.

The flotilla zigzagged in the dark, narrowly avoiding collision only through the remarkable skill of the boatmen. The light of the half moon and myriad stars was reflected on the tips of their oars as they dipped and sliced into the silvery water. The boats competed with each other to come alongside the vast hulls of the merchantmen where their passengers and luggage were hauled aboard by means of chairs, ropes, cranes and pulleys. Folk were afforded scant dignity, despite their age or gentility, in boarding a vessel in the Downs.

A mighty cacophony struck up as the merchantmen prepared for departure. There was the straining of ropes and the whipping of canvas as the triple or quadruple banks of sails were unfurled. There was the creaking of timbers as the ship rose and fell with the swell and the grinding of chains as the massive anchors were weighed. And there was the haunting chant of sea shanties as the crew laboured under the watchful eye of the captain. Finally, there was the booming of cannons as each ship departed, signalling a confident: 'Godspeed'.

By contrast, there was little noise from the professional sailors of the Royal Navy as they embarked in their longboats and pinnaces from the Navy Yard. On board the men-o'-war, the disciplined crew were trained to prepare for departure by directions from their bosun's shrill silver whistle. For the Royal Navy had already gained the reputation of being the 'silent service'. At last, they too fired their farewell salutes but with an uneven number of guns since an even number was reserved exclusively for a funeral at sea. Miraculously, four hundred sailing ships of the Royal and Merchant Navies departed without incident within the space of an hour from the world-renowned Downs Anchorage.

When all the excitement had died, down two isolated figures remained standing desolately on the foreshore. Mayor Powell, his head bowed in despair, realised that his religious fervour directed at preventing the boatmen from working on the Sabbath was a dismal failure. And Miles, convinced that it was he alone who had whistled up that high wind, was left wondering which one of those sailing ships was carrying Jenny's widowed father to distant lands, still dressed in his Sunday best clothes.

6

SEARCH

THE SKELETON rose from its coffin - bone by bone by bone - and began to stride purposefully along the dark, dingy tunnel towards the petrified boy. Contraband lay discarded all around - kegs of brandy, caskets of tea, packets of tobacco, bales of silk. Bands of lace slowly wound themselves around the skeleton as it marched relentlessly forward. It looked as if it was being dressed by invisible hands for a dance macabre at a mummy's ball.

Miles searched desperately for a place to hide but there was nowhere to be found along the damp, stone walls of the narrow tunnel.

Now he realised that the level of water in which he was standing was starting to rise. He was below sea level. It began with just a trickle and then turned into an almighty gush. Water was racing up to his knees, his waist and, rising still, it had almost reached his shoulders. He tried to swim but found he was being held down beneath the murky waves by the vengeful dipper from the bathing machine.

Above him, as he struggled for air, stacks of coffins started to lift from their marble shelves. They drifted and floated aimlessly on the heaving waves. They crashed into each other with a mighty thud. Their lids splintered so that their occupants began to rise, tumble out of their confinement and find a footing in their flooded vault. All around, skulls turned towards him and boney fingers pointed accusingly at Miles.

'You've found out our secret,' the jaws mouthed. 'We will have our revenge!'

Over the thunderous noise of the gushing water and the crashing coffins, the tunnel reverberated with the r a t t l i n g o f b o n e s.

Scratch. Scratch. . Scratch. . .

Miles woke with a start and sat bolt upright. Sweat poured from his sodden brow. He stared straight ahead and, almost with disbelief, took in the familiar surroundings. He rubbed his eyes vigorously trying to remove those terrifying images from his mind. He was back at the inn. . . back in his attic. . . back in the real world.

But the strange noise continued. Quieter now than before but just as persistent. A scraping sound came from inside the jib cupboard that served as his walk-in wardrobe. Still half asleep, he stumbled across the room to investigate, guessing that the culprit would be none other than that annoying cat.

Jinx did not spring out when he opened the door. Miles fumbled with the cloaks draped over their stout wooden pegs and the pairs of seamen's boots casually strewn on the floor. The cat was not there but the scratching continued.

What made Miles push the far wall of the wardrobe cannot be readily explained. But he did and it sprang back allowing the trapped cat to scamper out, its fur ruffled and its tongue hissing. Here, revealed, was an interior door giving access to a secret room. How could Miles resist exploring further?

It was only a tiny space, dark and square, but streaks of faint daylight filtered through the cracks of the rough pine wall panels. There were distorted sounds of angry voices coming from the other side of the end wall. When he pushed his face against these panels Miles could see through the narrow gaps and into the room on the other side. He was level with the private closet of Mr Mayor.

Here was a modest room with a pine dado above which was hung the most exquisite hand painted Chinese wallpaper. Charmingly, it featured a naturalistic landscape of exotic birds and butterflies flitting among orange blossoms. Mayor Powell had spared no expense in papering his own personal room. The recently introduced tax on each imported oriental roll must have cost a small fortune. At one time he had baulked at paying the obligatory sum of one penny per square yard for a cheaper wall hanging of stripes or checks but in his declining years he saw little problem in indulging himself, every now and then. . .

Miles could just see the Mayor slumped in a wide armchair, his feet on a low footstool, puffing a churchwarden pipe and sipping cherry cordial as a cure for his painful gout. A steaming silver coffee pot with a single cup was placed near to hand on a side table. He was wearing an ample powdering gown and his head was bare, revealing short, cropped hair. A manservant stood behind him dressing his fluffy white wig on a mahogany stand. But this was not the man whom the Mayor was addressing.

Despite his relaxed pose, the Mayor was clearly agitated. He was thumping the table so that the china cups on a silver tray were jumping up and down, like gymnasts on a trampoline. An unread newspaper fluttered onto the floor. His unseen visitor bent to pick it up.

'Leave that!'

Miles now recognised the man from the night before. It was Lieutenant Bray, smartly uniformed and politely mannered. He had exciting news to convey about the Revenue cutter, 'Scorpion', which had intercepted a local lugger, 'Diana', returning under cover of the cliffs at Dover. The officers involved had been acting upon information he, himself, had provided. They had boarded the overladen vessel - low in the water - and confiscated its illicit cargo. There had been feeble attempt by its crew to conceal literally scores of casks of brandy, rum and gin and also quantities of fine wines from France. Naturally, the Lieutenant was extremely pleased with himself.

But the Mayor was most displeased with him.

He bullied and harangued him in between his sips of coffee and puffs of baccy. For although the Royal Navy officer was himself a man of authority, dutiful and reliable, neither his training nor his experience had prepared him for confrontation with such a forcible personality as Deale's Mayor, Thomas Powell.

Lieutenant Gabriel Bray wore the uniform of a Regulating Officer. This consisted of a navy-blue jacket with white facings and brass buttons, a sour cream waistcoat, white pantaloons and silver buckled shoes. He wore a ginger curly wig under his tricorn hat. His smart attire belied the fact that he was born a humble countryman who had never yet ventured out to sea.

In truth, Gabriel Bray was short, stocky and stubborn as a

mule. He had pitted cheeks and buck teeth which caused him to froth and spit when excited. His most telling features were his sharp eyes and cruel lips. He was still young though keenly ambitious. He considered that his present unenviable position might yet stand him in good stead for eventual promotion by the Admiralty.

Lieutenant Bray was totally oblivious to other men's misery and this despicable trait allowed him to lead his team of ruffians to press men indiscriminately in this seaport. He was indefatigable in what he believed to be his bounden duty to King and Country, particularly in times of war, to forcibly recruit fit and able men into the service of the Royal Navy.

He had quickly learned the tricks of the trade.

It was common knowledge that there was no finer recruiting ground than the Downs. Here ships forgathered from every quarter of the navigable globe. Homebound merchantmen were prey to patrols of pressmen afloat that boarded these magnificent vessels the moment they swept in from the south. This had become Bray's jealously guarded territory.

He and his ruffians swooped aboard these merchantmen the moment they arrived and swiftly transferred their experienced sailors to nearby Royal Navy men-o'-war. Unlucky sailors, in this detestable manner, were returned immediately to sea without ever setting foot ashore or being united with their loving families.

Occasionally, Bray had been thwarted.

Sympathetic captains sometimes built hides within their ships for sailors to avoid detection. They then claimed that the remaining crew was necessary to navigate their ships around the Goodwin Sands. Wily captains also set sailors ashore further down the coast, at Rye, for instance, allowing them to escape across deserted Romney Marsh before they could be captured by press gangs from Folkestone or Dover.

At times, when a general press was ordered, the Lieutenant was forced to operate on dry land. There, Lieutenant Bray was certain to meet with violent resistance from a town's inhabitants.

Mistakenly, he had once entered the 'Noah's Ark' with his common press warrant and was confronted by landlord Lew. He insisted that he should have been previously informed of his intentions by the Regulating Officer and that the search for conscripts should only be executed officially by a Justice of the Peace.

He refused Bray entry beyond the taproom without a search warrant for the upstairs rooms. Unwisely, Bray drew his sword and allowed one of his ruffians to bloody Lew's nose with a blow from his pistol butt. Bray ordered his men to break down every door in the house if necessary, to locate any healthy single man that the inn might harbour.

His ruffians duly searched the premises and located five or six fit young men cowering in cupboards and wardrobes. They were dragged forcibly from their place of concealment. Meanwhile, Lew's wife, Gwen, had slipped out of the side door of the inn to summon aid from the boatmen and an affray erupted which was only halted by the arrival of the Chief Magistrate.

The Magistrate complained directly to the Admiralty that the Regulating Officer had acted illegally, and his objection was upheld. The culmination was that the man-o'-war was detained until the half dozen conscripts were returned unharmed to the seaport and Uncle Lew was awarded compensation for trespass, assault and wrongful arrest. The Admiralty had no wish to be presented as an inhumane service and the Magistrate was feted by the town.

It was that same Magistrate, Mayor Powell, who now confronted Lieutenant Bray in his private upstairs chamber.

Miles' view through the slits in the panels was naturally restricted. He could see the Mayor and his servant, but Lieutenant Bray came into sight infrequently. Miles slid down the wall and squatted on the floor of the secret room. He no longer had to strain to listen to their heated conversation because their voices became increasingly loud and aggressive.

And more and more animated.

'You seem to have usurped my authority, Lieutenant Bray.'

'In what way, I pray, Mr Mayor?'

'As Chief Magistrate, I claim the sole right to provide volunteer sailors in this port. You, sir, are charged with compelling experienced seamen to return into the service of the King's Navy. This, I might add, is an entitlement denied even to the Army.'

'My warrant allows me to enter the taverns and public houses,' countered the Lieutenant, 'to look for new recruits and also deserters but on that particular day you complain about, all their doors were firmly shut!'

'On my strict orders since it was the Sabbath! You should have confined your patrols to the open sea.'

'The Downs Anchorage has been becalmed for weeks, as well you know, Mr. Mayor. There has been no merchantmen entering the port for all of that time. My men. . .'

'Ruffians!'

'. . . were forced to scour the seafront which also appeared deserted on that particular day.'

'The boatmen were working on a Sunday. I dismissed them all to their homes. There they could spend time more worthily with their own family and at their devotions.'

Mayor Powell was not used to having his authority challenged. He continued thumping the table with increasing force so that the entire coffee service - cups, jugs and bowls - was now in imminent peril.

His manservant - courageously, considering the circumstances - decided this was the moment to intervene between the two sparring men. He slipped a newly dressed formal wig over the Mayor's balding pate and began adjusting it. He snipped off a curl, singed when his master had dozed too near a candle flame. There was now competition for attention from the Mayor between the dressed wig and the distressed Lieutenant.

Lieutenant Bray decided to pursue the defence of his actions on a different tact. He inclined his head respectfully, wrung his hands in subjection but revealed the first signs of nervousness by slightly frothing at the sides of his mouth.

'Mr Mayor, I found only one boatman on the beach that day and he was not carrying a ticket of exemption so I know he could not be a pilot offering valuable service to the fleet.'

The Mayor impatiently brushed the servant's comb aside as he attempted minute adjustments to the fulsome wig.

'Lieutenant Bray, my neighbour, Mr Hubbard, is neither a boatman nor a pilot. His limp, you must observe, will not allow him to be at sea for lengthy periods. He cannot keep his balance on a swaying deck! He is simply a shopkeeper who deals in second-hand clothes - 'slops', if you prefer - to our very own mariners. And he is a hardworking and trustworthy tradesman at that!'

In the moment of silence, the dedicated wig dressing was resumed. A hand mirror was held in front of the Mayor for his Worship's approval of the reflected image. Alas, this was but the calm before the storm.

'If he is a bachelor then he is still eligible for service,' ventured the Lieutenant.

'Fiddlesticks!' raged the Mayor.

The hand mirror took flight across the room as the Mayor knocked it from his servant's hand.

'Mr Hubbard is a married man and a homeowner with a young daughter to care for. His wife died in childbirth and he has dedicated his life to looking after his only child. Jenny is her name, and she has now been left desolate.'

Mayor Powell was now glaring at Lieutenant Bray with the same fixed stare that had silenced an entire congregation in church that very Sunday.

'Perhaps I may add, if you care to listen, I set John Hubbard up in business in his slops shop myself.'

Unabashed, the Lieutenant continued his protestations. Was he brave or was he foolish?

'There is nothing I can do further, Mr Mayor, for Mr Hubbard's ship has now sailed. He will be detained in service until the time when he is paid off. . . but only after he has finished his present term of duty.'

Tentatively, the manservant attempted to powder the now skew-whiff wig with a pair of miniature bellows.

'Careful with that,' mumbled the Mayor. 'Mr Pitt has just

introduced a tax on hair powder. Lord knows how long we will be able to afford to have our wigs dressed and powdered. We will soon have to resort to wearing our normal head of hair and go about like hedgepigs.'

And having addressed the final sentence to posterity, the Mayor turned his attention once more to demeaning the luckless Lieutenant.

'Lieutenant Bray, you will contact Mr Hubbard's ship before it sails beyond Dover and return him to his home and daughter. You forget one thing. If your purpose in being overzealous in your duty to your King and country allows you to consider that you will gain easy promotion through the ranks you will think again. The Mayor of Deale is not only Chief Magistrate, but by tradition, the moment he boards a Royal Navy ship in the Downs he automatically assumes the rank of Admiral.'

There was little chance that the conflict might continue. The manservant, inadvertently, resolved the dispute. By powdering the wig too intensely, he set up a thick aromatic smoke screen that set the Mayor and the Lieutenant violently sneezing. And Miles, hidden beyond the wall almost gave the game away by collapsing in a fit of uncontrollable giggles.

It was a peculiarity of the 'Noah's Ark' inn that it experienced a mini eclipse around midday.

This was caused by the fact that the sun, travelling from east to west, passed directly overhead for approximately two hours, either side of noon. As all the windows of the inn faced in both these directions, it rendered the interior of the house disconcertingly dark, even in daytime.

For those few hours the inn, itself, enjoyed a quiet period. Hired coaches left for London via Dover in the early morning and returned in the late afternoon with fresh travellers seeking overnight accommodation before their ship sailed. Boatmen, who were not patrolling the Channel, preferred to take their refreshment in the evenings.

Servants were making beds in the upstairs chambers, polishing the mirrors on the landing, sweeping the hearths in the kitchen or beating carpets in the backyard. Uncle Lew was checking his accounts in his counting house and Aunt Gwen was supervising the restocking of the kitchen larder.

So, then, the body of the inn remained deserted, almost always, around midday. Time, Miles guessed, to explore and search for tunnels. The most obvious place to look was in the cellar.

No one noticed as he took a candle and slipped into the taproom. He ducked down behind the bar and lifted the trap door by its iron ring. There was a short flight of wooden steps down which Miles was careful to descend, sailor fashion, backwards.

The cellar was lighter than he expected owing to the fact that wintry sunlight strayed from the chute grille on street level where the barrels were shunted by the draymen. Anyway, his eyes soon adjusted so that he could see clearly along the long underground room with its short passages leading off on either side.

Great wooden casks loomed overhead, stacked on their sturdy stands, and cobwebs trailed across the beams that had split under the weight of the rafters they supported. Although the floor was paved there were puddles of salt water which Miles stepped over and several times, he had to bend almost double, even though he was only a boy, to negotiate the sequence of arches that separated the exceedingly long passage of the dismal cellar. Overall, there was the heady aroma of hops from the casked beer and ale.

Miles paused to light his candle before he entered one of the shorter passages which he was convinced might lead to the start of a smugglers' tunnel. It was like, he imagined, exploring the crypt in a church. Just as dark and creepy. And as scary.

He felt the far wall in the barrel-vaulted chamber. It was damp to his touch. Water trickled down the surface. He felt all around, thinking himself daring, but there was no sign of any entrance to a tunnel. The way ahead was firmly blocked.

Then something scampered across his feet and he cried out as he stumbled. The candle dropped to the floor and was extinguished in a puddle. He turned around and made his way back, feeling against the rough brick walls until he came again to the main passage. He rubbed his eyes as the natural light hit him.

He stood level with a pair of thick leather boots.

Perched on the steps in front of him was Uncle Lew, toying with a tankard and stroking his stubbly chin. A look of triumph swept across his face. 'Happy now?'

Uncle Lew ducked his head as he descended further. He strolled over to a cask and swivelled its tap. He filled his tankard with a lively froth. 'Looking for something, were you, my inquisitive little nephew, down from London? Do tell your favourite uncle. . . all.'

And he sat down on an upturned barrel, smiled and waited for Miles' awkward explanation.

Miles shivered. He realised, not for the first time, that he was afraid of his uncle. Although he never threatened violence, the tone of his voice held certain menace. He remembered his mother had told him, illogically, she never trusted a man with a gap in his front teeth!

Miles hesitated. "I was looking for. . .'

'Smugglers,' supplied his Uncle. 'Now where do you suppose their tunnels - supposing they exist - might be? Not underground, I warrant. Think hard. You are an intelligent boy, or so your Aunt tells me. I am yet to be convinced!'

Uncle Lew explained, reasonably enough, that it would be impossible to construct an underground tunnel so close to the seafront. The cellar of the inn was built on shingle, below sea level. Water always found its own level and on an exceptional high tide would rise up through the shingle and swamp the cellars. That was why the beer and ale casks were stacked high above the ground.

Miles saw the sense of this but did not quite understand why his uncle was taking such pains to explain it to him.

Uncle Lew persisted by posing several questions. Where was the machinery capable of boring a tunnel underground? How could engineers shore up the walls against collapse? What would happen to the huge amount of surplus shingle that was inevitably dug out? A giveaway, surely, if an army of labourers with wheelbarrows were to be seen conveying load upon load of pebbles back up the beach!

Miles was drawn into the discussion. For the first timed found that he could communicate on equal terms with his uncle. 'But I have often overheard. . . in London. . . that Deale is riddled with tunnels. They lead to the church. . . the castle. . . the seafront!'

'Rumours abound, my boy.' He offered his nephew a sip of ale. It was his first friendly gesture. Miles refused. He did not know why.

'That's not to say there might well be a tunnel,' Uncle Lew conceded. 'But they ain't below deck in my inn, that's for sure. First place the Revenue Men would think to look.'

And now Uncle Lew turned and stared hard at his nephew. He lowered his tone as he drew him into the often-rehearsed tale of the officer who uncovered a smugglers' tunnel. Unwisely, he entered it alone and became trapped inside. Anyone who entered afterwards would be warned of danger by the rattling of his skeletal bones. . .

Impressed by the telling of his own tale, Lew took a last sip of ale and plonked his empty tankard on top of a tall cask. That moment a great brown rat scurried past. Jinx darted out from his hiding place from behind a beer barrel, knocked over the pewter tankard and chased his squealing prey into the darkness!

It was Lew's turn to be taken unawares. 'Drat that cat!' he exploded. 'He's here, there and everywhere!' He examined a bleeding cut on his elbow. 'He's worse even than that accursed Scarlet Pimpernel!'

Daylight was dying fast as Captain Cannons led his reinforcements of dragoons from Canterbury though the cobbled streets of Deale. They were smartly uniformed and strictly disciplined. Privately, they were tired, hungry and more than a little apprehensive about securing suitable billets.

The Captain halted at the 'Noah's Ark' and dismounted. A dragoon held the reins of his hunter as he entered the inn.

He took off his gloves and held them loosely in his hand as he called out for the landlord. Lew appeared in the passage to confront the Captain of Dragoons.

'What can we do for you, Captain?' he enquired, suspiciously.

'My men, sir, require good beds for the night.'

'I'm afraid, Captain, that is out of the question.' Lew squared up and prepared for battle. 'Surely you are comfortably accommodated in the barn I've rented out to you and your men on the Sandhills.'

'Landlord, it is not comfort I am seeking but security for my men while they are about the King's business.' The Captain's voice was cold. 'Besides, your charges there are exorbitant. There are rooms, here, I vow at a fraction of the price you charge for that ramshackle outhouse you call a barn.'

'I regret to inform you, that all my rooms are taken.'

'Nonsense, Sir.' The captain gave a vicious swipe with the gloves across his own hand. 'Everyone knows that an entire fleet of merchant ships sailed last night. You cannot have filled your guest rooms already. Why, I note that the evening coach has not yet arrived from Dover?'

Lew shrugged aside these comments while he obstinately blocked the way through the passage.

'Stand aside, Landlord, while my men search these premises.' He hailed his troops for support. 'We shall test the veracity of your statement.'

Half a dozen eager soldiers stormed the passage, brushing Lew to one side, and burst open the door that led from the passage. They rushed up the flight of stairs and onto the open landing. The clattering of their boots resounded through the inn, pounding the floorboards and rattling the windows.

The Captain was confident of the outcome of his unannounced search. He stood with firm resolution. His face was impassive. Lew merely smirked.

Captain Cannons of the Light Dragoons relied upon intelligence from his trained scouts and voluntary informers. He had calculated, in any case, that the port's inns and taverns had emptied the moment the merchant fleet had sailed. He had acted swiftly by ordering his troops to scour the town for appropriate lodgings.

Alas, neither his scouts nor informers were a match for the town's secret telegraph that forewarned the landlords and hoteliers that his dragoons were intending to march through the streets in search of billets. Uncle Lew had earlier received a scribbled note, attached to the leg of a carrier pigeon that landed at an open dormer window on the top floor, informing him of Captain Cannons' intentions.

Meanwhile, the servants at the 'Noah's Ark' retreated the moment they sensed danger. Some hid in cupboards; others under beds. The less timorous positioned themselves against the cheap whitewashed walls of the corridors as the troops pushed past, kicking locked doors open and forcing entry into each of the private chambers.

Every room held a surprise!

Widow Ducker held a slither of towelling to her plump, naked body as she prepared to step into a scolding hip bath. She did not scream or hide behind the screen as the young soldier burst open her chamber door. She made not the slightest attempt to protect her modesty. Rather, she winked, alluringly, at him through the steam. The soldier's face turned bright crimson as he retreated swiftly from her ample presence.

An equally alarming sight was met by the soldier who turned the handle of the door opposite. Bones, the highwayman, had tucked himself into a truckle bed with just his blistered, bunioned feet poked out from underneath bare boards. His body was wound in a grubby, threadbare cloth so that he resembled a cadaver cocooned in his shroud. It looked like an indifferent undertaker had stowed away a body for burial at a later date for want of a coffin and mourners. The soldier closed the door, reverently almost, not wanting to summon up spectres by waking the dead.

A third bedroom revealed the figure of a plump coachman stretched out across a lumpy, bumpy bed. His greatcoat covered his body; his hat, gloves and whip rested against the splintered pine headboard. In a cracked jug on a bedside table was a fresh nosegay of papery asters that struggled to scent the fetid chamber. They were, alas, doomed to failure since there was an overpowering smell of soiled boots, damp hay and horse manure. When the slumbering figure opened his mouth to snore it resembled an enormous rat trap. The dragoon, firmly holding his nose, closed the door leaving Goggins to reverse back into the Land of Nod.

The last bedroom on this first floor was situated at the front of the house. The soldier peered cautiously around the ill lit room. It appeared to be empty until he spotted in the dimness a single box bed against the far wall. The moonlight revealed the mound of a sleeping figure under a patchwork quilt. He could not tell whether it was male or female but when he approached it a cork leg brushed against his thigh. As he stumbled backwards with surprise, he set in motion a rocking chair. He fought to regain his balance. Then something small and eerie darted along the top of the wooden frame which made the new recruit react with terror. In an unearthly voice it shrilly squeaked: 'Man overboard!'

And in the attic bedroom the soldiers found a small boy sitting on the edge of his bed, staring into space and idly passing a brass bed knob to and fro between his cupped hands. He turned and looked at them with dismay. Miles's thoughts were miles away. He was reflecting, at his tender age, of the trouble that he had inadvertently caused his relatives. And of the wisdom of informing Captain Cannons of his strong chance of securing billets at the 'Noah's Ark', now that the merchant fleets had sailed.

Outwitted! Captain Cannons was furious that he had been out manoeuvred by a common seaside landlord. A blazing row erupted between the two men two flights down in the street below. Evidently, the Captain of Dragoons was not yet prepared to concede defeat. He reminded the landlord that, since he was not able to provide lodgings for his troops or indeed any prospective customers, he was obliged by law to remove his sign.

As Miles tucked himself into bed that evening, he recalled the strenuous effort - and the curses - as Uncle Lew mounted a tall wooden ladder and unhooked the inn sign, precariously by lamplight, to announce to this mysterious seaport: 'House Full'.

7

HIDE

IT IS AMAZING how you can go to bed with a problem and when you wake in the morning it has been solved! Your brain, it seems, works overtime while you are asleep. Where *is* that elusive smugglers' tunnel? Miles woke, bright and bold, and bounced out of bed with a plan of action. It seemed so obvious. Why hadn't he thought of it before?

Then, again, it hardly made sense. No sense at all. But worth a try. That fire that was never lit!

Miles would wait once again until the taproom was empty around late morning for him to creep through the right-hand door to search the brick chimney in the deserted public room across the passage. He was exhilarated by the thought of his brilliant idea. The unused chimney could hardly be clogged with soot. There were no chimney pots and so his exit would be clear. It would be down to sheer tenacity to reach the top and maybe locate a secret door built into the brickwork.

There was no need, for sure, to be particular about washing and dressing, thought Miles. This was to be a morning devoted entirely to exploration!

As he crept along the short passage between the inn's two rooms, he heard lowered voices coming from the taproom. He was in stockinged feet and carrying his shoes, so he knew he had not, himself, been heard. He paused to listen. Aunt Gwen was telling one of the serving girls about an unfortunate event that had happened early that very morning.

Apparently, Mr. Goggins had been apprehended as he travelled along the Ancient Highway towards Canterbury via Sandwich by two Revenue Men. They had searched his coach and found a quantity of Chantilly silk and Valenciennes lace stowed under the seat inside. Mr Goggins had been arrested, he had been taken to the town gaol and his vehicle had been confiscated. He swore on his life that he had not known a thing about the origin of the contents of his carriage but that he was merely doing his sweetheart, Nancy, a favour in returning unwanted presents!

The ladies began to giggle. Miles took this as an opportunity to proceed to the cold snug. He guessed their secret would be known throughout the whole town before noon.

As he replaced his shoes his thoughts strayed to home and the end of summer when the chimneys of his family riverside home, 'Hartover', along Chiswick Mall, were cleaned by the itinerant sweeper. 'Grimes', his mother called him, but that, he thought, was a reference, not to his actual name but to his appearance. His timely visit heralded the approach of winter and preparation for warmth and security. For Miles, it was also the promise of fireside activities: baking apples, toasting muffins and roasting chestnuts.

Mr Grimes appeared each time with a different apprentice. Fresh from the workhouse and usually an orphan. What happened to the old one set the family an amusing puzzle around the breakfast table? They relished their guessing games.

Had the last lad had a fall? Was he still stuck up a flue? Or was his skeleton trapped in their own chimney? These speculations were frightful, to be sure, but of little concern to the family who greatly prized their home comforts.

After a while they became bored with this conundrum and ceased to care. For, lo and behold, the very next autumn there was Mr. Grimes, regular as clockwork, with a brand new boy! He would be struggling to offload the brushes from the donkey cart and, returning after the job was done, burdened with sackfuls of soot. His master's sole concession to assistance was to secure sheets of strong brown paper over the fireplace to catch fallen soot while dispatching his novice, armed with a bristle brush tied to his wrist, to attack their tall, twisting chimneys. A mammoth task!

The pompous sweep swelled with pride as he regaled the master or mistress of the house, or indeed anyone who cared to listen to him, of his charitable disposition in setting up a young apprentice with a noble career that would last him a lifetime.

Each autumn, Miles and his mother would gather on their leaf strewn lawn to watch for the sweep's brush to appear in turn at the top of each of their own ornate chimneys. They were often joined by their estate manager, head gardener and gate keeper who stood in an admiring circle. Mr Grimes enjoyed their attention. He felt like a ringmaster at a circus.

He stood patting his paunch and sniffing the air. While his apprentice cleaned soot from his clients' chimneys, he would block his own crooked chimney with a pinch of snuff. He would then - after much sneezing and wheezing - expound his innovative methods of training his army of apprentices.

Mr Grimes would light a fire in the grate, he confided, which would send a hesitant boy further up the flue in search of air to breathe. 'Boys is wery obstinit,' pronounced the portly sage, 'and wery lazy. There's nothink like a good hot blaze to make 'em climb up wiv a start!' Interpreting Miles' mother's stunned silence as approval he continued extolling the virtues of his novel tutoring. 'It's 'umane, too, a'cause, even if they've stuck in the chimbley, roasting of their feet makes 'em struggle to h'extricate themselves.'

Miles' mother gave a sigh of relief when the new boy at last reappeared above their rooftop although his features were obliterated by coal dust. He looked like a mole startled by his sudden emergence from the soil. Mr Grimes consulted his pocket watch and knotted his spotted kerchief. He tossed a carrot to his mangy donkey in return for her patience and tousled the shivering boy's hair as a reward for his labour.

'A shillin' if yew plez, marm, per chimbly.' Tapping his cap as a mark of respect, he bade a cheery farewell. This benevolent taskmaster then hauled his barefoot apprentice - whose name may have been 'Ruff', 'Tuff' or 'Scruff' - onto his cart where he was left to make a cushion from the discarded soot bags.

Mr Grimes broke into a doleful song as the donkey trotted and the cart trundled along the riverbank towards the neighbouring village:

> 'When my mother died I was very young,
> And my father sold me while yet my tongue
> Could scarcely cry: 'Weep, weep, weep, weep!'
> So your chimneys I sweep and in soot I sleep.'

Miles, in his ignorance, envied the boys who never washed themselves or changed their clothes while before them lay a life of pure excitement. They did not have to learn from boring books in musty schoolrooms but were free to participate in their own adventures. Now it was his turn to attempt a self-imposed challenge and scale the dizzy heights of the inn's own 'chimbly'. He surveyed the stone hearth and peered up the wide sweep of the chimney flue to view the open sky and the iron rungs where the chimney boys climbed.

Halfway up the chimney it occurred to Miles that, maybe, this was not such a good idea.

He was, after all, attempting to climb the equivalent of a two storey building. But from the inside. The golden rule, or so he believed, was never, ever to look down. The truth was that he could not see his feet even if he wanted to because it was impossible for him to turn his head and peer downwards. The light was sorely restricted in the dark, tight flue. His only option was to keep travelling towards that tiny square of precious daylight ahead.

Grimes' grim tales began to worry him.

There was that time when a boy became stuck, and his master poured water down through the pots to dislodge him. Another time, he sent a second lad up with a rope to tie it to a stranded boy's foot and tug him down. Both episodes ended in disaster. Yet again, Grimes sent for workmen to knock a hole in the bricks and haul one terrified infant through the aperture. Thankfully, these horrendous incidents could not now be repeated because - and here was a gruesome thought - no one knew Miles was there! If he did not want to be incarcerated forever, he must control his fear and continue to climb.

Miles had been taking a precarious rest with his feet on one rung and his hands on another, further up the constricted funnel of the chimney. He took a deep breath and resumed his ascent. His knees and his elbows were scuffed as he propelled himself painfully onwards and upwards. Despite aching fatigue, he resolved upon this sudden final spurt. Deftly, now, he cater-pillared his way to the top.

He had grossly misjudged the state of the chimney. The climb was far more difficult than he had anticipated. His face was blackened with coal soot. . . his eyes were reddened with brick dust. . . his knuckles whitened with tension. His nose was blocked and his mouth dry. His elbows and knees were raw from scuffing by the rough-hewn walls. He felt he was suffocating. . . when at last he reached the summit.

His head popped out like a Jack-in-the box.

Miles clung with his tight fists before making that final push to climb out and over the stack. He bent double and choked in air. He stood balancing on the hip tiles and surveyed the russet rooftops. Seagulls were warming their bottoms on the smoking chimney pots; brown rats were scurrying along the narrow gullies. Then he stared ahead in disbelief.

He had found the entrance to the tunnel.

The roof of the 'Noah's Ark' was double hipped. This meant that the valley in between the steep parallel roofs was concealed from view at ground level. Anyone who ventured upon the rooftops could carry on their activities completely unobserved from front and back.

A thought entered Miles's head. Perhaps someone was working on the rooftop that fateful day when a tile was dislodged. The one that came crashing down to the street and narrowly missed Captain Cannons? Maybe, even, the tile was sent spinning down deliberately to frighten, injure or maim that meddlesome Dragoon?

Tucked alongside the far chimney stack - the one belching smoke - was a set of stone steps. They led down to the crumbling brick back wall of the corner house which was the first of the long line of properties whose rooftops higgled and piggled their way towards the seafront.

At the base of the crudely cut steps was a weathered wooden trapdoor. It opened, but only after persistent pushes. Miles scrambled through and entered a tight roof space. The ceiling was too low for him to stand and his hunched shoulders brushed against cobwebs. Miles realised he was trespassing upon the residence of Mayor Powell. However, the Magistrate would never know of his presence because the roof space was completely sealed, apart from the exterior trapdoor.

When his eyes adjusted to the half-light he could see perfectly clearly. To his left there was a wide opening between timber struts. This invited further investigation. What lay ahead was a series of connecting cramped attics with heavy beams. There was still no sign of any access for the householders living below. The secret store stretched out forever. Each linked attic was crammed with contraband.

Here was a veritable Aladdin's cave!

Kegs of spirits were stored from floor to ceiling, more than enough to supply the whole town with intoxicating liquor.

Their contents were chalked on the circular timber sides - brandy, rum and Dutch Geneva that was simply marked 'gin'. Perhaps these were from the bathing machine that Miles had discovered in the night? Brandy, Miles knew, was colourless - he had noticed the customers drink it at the inn - but its distinctive honey tincture would have been added once the duty had been paid to the Customs officials.

Stored separately in an adjoining attic, protected from direct sunlight, were sumptuous dress materials, enough to furnish a fashionable London emporium. Piled high were crisscrossed rolls of luxury velvets, damasks, satins, silks, gold and silver brocade, waiting to be purchased, transported and worked into dazzling garments by experienced dressmakers for ladies of quality in London. Half opened boxes of costume accessories - ribbons, laces, ostrich plumes, bead purses, silk slippers, leather gloves, ivory fans - were casually heaped against the leaning walls. Their colourful contents, spilling onto the dusty floorboards, would be the envy of any member of the Georgian court circle.

Nearby, packing cases revealed a cornucopia of curiosities - scented snuff, sealing wax, hair powder, washing soap, dried fruits, playing cards. There were packs of starch for seamstresses to stiffen blouses and bundles of straw for milliners to weave into bonnets. There were sealed boxes of raw coffee, rich cocoa and bittersweet chocolate. Miles continued to rummage and found a further assortment of objects - dice, wire, paper, nails, currants, counterpanes, even coconuts…He recognised instantly that there were valuable commodities, untaxed but available at knockdown prices from the anonymous owners of this vast arial storehouse.

At the far end of this rambling rooftop run was an open square shaft, sawn roughly into the thick floorboards. Attached to a beam above it was a pulley with a strong rope and iron hook. Evidently, this was the winding gear for raising the goods from the cellar, three flights below. The shaft, Miles knew - because he had seen it - passed down through the seafront corner shop owned by Jenny and her father.

They must both have known the secret of the tunnel all along.

Miles lay on his tummy and peered into the abyss. He lacked a lantern to lower into the shaft. Its light might reveal further surprises. Perhaps trapdoors in the rooms above the shop. He had never before experienced such a thrill of discovery. And he had convinced himself that at his young age he had conquered all his fears of adventure.

That was until he heard the r a t t l i n g   o f   b o n e s!

The unearthly sound came from the furthest attic where he had entered the rooftop tunnel.

He could track the skeleton as it raced towards him. It thudded and thundered, pounced and pounded, clattered and clanked on the bare boards. It knocked boxes and bales over as it tore through the rooms. Ruthlessly, relentlessly, it sped towards him in search of its vulnerable prey.

Miles reacted quickly and dived behind a row of barrels. He crunched up, tightly, hoping that the ghostly fiend might overlook him. Nervously, he peeped through the narrow gap between two barrels. However, could he, a mere boy, defend himself against something supernatural?

His heart was pounding. He had studied the human skeleton his tutor kept in the corner of his schoolroom. He could identify the sequence of bones – toe... foot... ankle... leg... knee... thigh... hip... back... shoulder... neck... head - as they creaked and cranked. And he could visualise the soulless skull with its grisly jaw and grinding teeth and ghastly eye sockets. All these dry bones had now come to life to haunt him and he was terrified.

And then. . . then it was all over!

Miles' imagination had worked overtime. Thoughts had jingled in his brain. There was the skeleton. There was the spectre. And he felt ashamed of his terror. Perched above him, having leapt onto the topmost barrel, was Jinx the cat. Attached to his rough fur was a necklace of scallop shells.

Miles whistled with sheer relief. He had been duped by his friends. They had planted wildly improbable stories into his susceptible mind. He had believed their tales implicitly. The clunking of the seashells in flight had conjured up visions of unearthly horrors.

He was vexed by his own gullibility. Then he rolled over onto his back and laughed and laughed as the cat's rough tongue licked the beads of sweat from his forehead.

Miles, still nursing his abrased knees after his morning's escapade, hobbled round the corner of Middle Street. His purpose was to locate Captain Cannons and inform him of his startling discovery. Immediately, he was swallowed up by groups of excited inhabitants who spared not a glance at his bruised and bloodied knees because they, too, were intent on heading for the beach.

As Miles scuttled along Silver Street, Mayor Powell stomped out of his front door, huffing and puffing, quite apoplectic. He turned and hurried in the same direction, still fastening his cloak, with his manservant close behind him, holding out at arm's length his powdered fluffy, white wig.

Along the seafront Miles was presented with an extraordinary scene. A veritable army of townsfolk had already assembled. They stood several rows deep and jostled for position. Men were riding along the foreshore, peering out of their carriages; women were pausing in their housework, leaning out of their windows. Boatmen were there in profusion standing on the steps of their huts, climbing on tubs and balancing on capstans. Miles thought at first it would be impossible for him to even glimpse what was going on but, being a resourceful boy, he slipped through the legs of an elderly mariner. His portly wife hit him hard on the backside with her furled umbrella.

Evidently, the dragoons were preparing for manoeuvres. The whole company was out in force. They were preventing the hordes of spectators from converging on the shingle. A few troops were mounted, and these were stationed at strategic points all along the coast. The troops were armed with either drawn sabres or loaded muskets. The air was full of anticipation. Napoleon's invasion must surely be imminent!

Captain Cannons was easy to identify. He was demonstrating supreme authority over his disciplined men. He was also exercising complete control over the unruly townsfolk, agog with curiosity. He rode to and fro along the beach giving orders and directions to all and sundry. Perhaps Miles was unwise to approach him the instant his friend rode by?

'Captain, I have found the tunnel. It's not where you'd think. And it's piled high with contraband. Everything you could think of! It starts at. . .' He stopped mid-sentence and found he was pointing directly at Jenny's corner shop. With dismay, he realised he was about to betray his friend. Fortunately, this was one of those moments when adults, however indulgent they might be towards young people, are not in any mood to pay wholehearted attention. Miles was aware at this moment he was just one of the crowd.

'Another time, laddie,' snapped the Captain. 'First, I have to deal with this lawless town.' He spurred his mount and rode away.

Miles, for the first time, was relieved that he had been brushed aside. Satisfied, at least, that he had not revealed too much, he turned seawards and surveyed the scene. The magnificent luggers were hauled up high onto the shingle on account of the spring tide. They presented a noble fleet - twenty, perhaps even thirty boats - stretching almost from castle to castle. In the spaces between them were the fabled galleys of varying lengths and number of oars. Strangely, Miles noticed, the dragoons had separated the boatmen from their craft. Whatever could be their purpose?

As Miles watched half a dozen Royal Navy cutters - manned and armed - swept into the Downs. Smaller, lighter than the 'Greyhound', they would have been drafted in from neighbouring ports - Dover, Folkestone, perhaps even Rye - to take part in this routine exercise. Their presence, though, seemed ominous. Miles could decipher several of their names without the aid of a spyglass - 'Viper', 'Hornet', 'Bee' - as they rode a short distance from the shore. It might have occurred to him that all these ships were named after creatures that carried a sting. Perhaps this should have given him a clue to the true motive of their presence that fateful forenoon.

Prominent was the 'Scorpion', with the stocky figure of her belligerent commander, Lieutenant Gabriel Bray, at her prow. He had been given charge of manoeuvres at sea. His own slick craft was weaving around and among those companion revenue vessels. He was carefully positioning them, with the aid of flags and signals, equidistant from each other, right along the shoreline. Obviously, they, too, were being prepared for engagement in this mock assault.

But several things did not ring true with Miles. For instance, these ships seemed too close inshore to repulse invaders from the open sea but were stationed, more, to defend the beach itself from attack. Revenue cutters were built, he knew, for the purpose of pursuit rather than warfare. Then again, the dragoons were making no attempt to conceal themselves as they would if they were really under threat. They were not turned seawards but instead faced inland as though they intended to fire their weapons upon the inhabitants themselves. And whatever could be the purpose of so many lighted bonfires on the beach in broad daylight? Surely, in the eventuality of an actual invasion, this would give their position away to the enemy. Nothing, to Miles, made any sense.

Then Lieutenant Bray fired a signal from the prow and in that second everything became crystal clear.

This was to be an act of retribution. Revenge for the rogue lugger, 'Diana', apprehended for her clandestine activities under the shadow of the White Cliffs. . . revenge for the crew of 'The Strawberry' who successfully evaded pursuit by the 'Greyhound'.. revenge, even, for Mr Goggins who attempted to transport contraband by his post coach to Canterbury. Captain Cannons was adamant that he would fulfil his duty in stamping out the nocturnal trade in Deale. A trade that unlawfully and audaciously denied the British Government of vast funds for the war effort in repelling a threatened invasion by revolutionary France.

This coordinated reprisal - about to be played out in the presence of the whole town - had been organised jointly by Captain Cannons and Lieutenant Bray. Yet it smacked of the highest authority in the land. That of the Prime Minister, William Pitt, who, as Lord Warden, was at that very moment safely ensconced in his fortress, the castle at Walmer.

On command, an assigned trooper marched over to a bonfire

and pulled out a burning stake. Holding it well away from his face, he hurled the flare high in the air so that it landed in the open hull of one of the larger luggers, 'Briton's Pride'. The crowd gasped as it set light to the great parchment coloured lug sail hoisted in preparation for a piloting expedition. The fire rapidly spread so that the whole craft - planked seats, wooden spars, canvas sails and even the sturdy cuddy where the crew had stored their rations in preparation for a prolonged trip - were engulfed in flames.

Amid the crackling timbers and the spitting oilcloths arose a mighty moan from the townsfolk watching in dismay as one of the finest luggers on the east coast was deliberately ignited. Flames rose high and sparks spat wide. The intense heat kept the desperate crew at a distance so that they were unable to attempt the rescue of their burning beach craft. Smoke stung their eyes, already stained with tears of anger and frustration. In minutes, the huge hull of their working lugger - Deale's pride and joy - was reduced to a smouldering heap of charred, tarred timber.

This devastating act was repeated right along the beach - troops first pouring pitch over a vessel to ensure it burned rapidly - a planned and deliberate example of public vandalism.

In this way a noble fleet of local luggers - 'Young England', 'Seaman's Glory', 'Pride of the Ocean'. 'Guiding Star' - was reduced to smouldering rubble. The furious boatmen surged forward at every fresh attempt at arson, but they were restrained from further action by volleys fired into the air by the dragoons. The troops then held their muskets firmly across their chest to form a barricade to prevent the hostile crowd from storming the beach. In retaliation the boatmen lobbed sticks and stones, but the tight military formation held and in less than an hour the incomprehensible and irreparable damage was complete.

Crews from the Royal Navy cutters manned their gigs and rowed towards the shore. Less effectively, they either tried to tow the galleys out into deep water and scuttle them or stove in their hulls with hatchets as they stood on the beach to render them unseaworthy. But the noble craft bobbed resiliently under the waves and being made of wood, naturally refused to sink. There was some faint hope, at least, of retrieving and repairing them at a later date.

Miles watched these appalling scenes in abject dismay. He could hardly believe what he had witnessed. Before his very eyes an entire fleet of working boats had been torched. All along the beach the carcasses of the splendid luggers were enveloped in thick black smoke which wafted relentlessly out and over the Downs. The jubilant crews of the revenue cutters fired a victory round before departing from the anchorage. They were soon lost to sight in the English Channel.

'Now about that secret tunnel…?'

Miles, roused from his reverie, turned and look upwards through the smoky haze. Captain Cannons leaned down from his high horse and smiled benignly. His face, his wig, his helmet, his uniform all remained impossibly pristine. It was as though he had no actual involvement in the recent barbarity. There was not a smear on his cheeks nor sweat on his brow. There was a complete absence of emotion on his face. Yet despite his tender years, Miles could read into its malice and malevolence.

'The tunnel, Miles?'

The whole scene on the beach now presented the carnage of a battlefield. Miles had gained first-hand an experience of mindless cruelty by responsible adults. The cinders settled, the horses whinnied, the crowds gasped in abject despair.

Miles turned and ducked under the mass of angry boatmen - with their raised arms and clenched fists - to slip away, appalled by his witnessing this almighty hullaballoo.

That evening Miles decided to call in at the corner shop and speak with Jenny. The door was shut, and the shop was closed. But that was just as he would expect after the day's traumas and the disturbances along the seafront. He noticed, too, that long pole was devoid of washing hung out to dry!

The parlour above the shop was still dimly lit with lamps and candles so Jenny was definitely at home although not answering the door. He threw pebbles up at the large bay window to attract her attention. Seconds later he heard her slippered feet patter down the stairs and the bolts turn from inside the shop door. She opened it a fraction and peered through the crack. Just enough for Jinx to slip out into the street. She beckoned Miles inside but then put her finger to her lips to signal that he was to keep quiet. He followed her up the winding stair.

Miles had a pleasant surprise when he tiptoed into the parlour. There, stretched out on a sofa, was Jenny's father. He was still dressed in his Sunday clothes, but a blanket was thrown over him and his stockinged feet were resting on a cushioned footstool.

'He walked over from Dover,' Jenny whispered. 'He's dead beat and I don't want him disturbed.'

She was a mite tearful and dabbed her eyes with a kerchief. She poured Miles a glass of ginger beer and handed it to him without a word. She smiled at him and he could sense her joy.

'I think you will find Mayor Powell was responsible for his release,' Miles surmised. 'For all his faults he is basically a kind man.'

Jenny nodded and sipped her drink. Miles was toying with his glass. His eyes were adjusting to the dimness of the little parlour.

'Jenny, I know the whereabouts of the smuggler's tunnel. I know where the contraband went when it left the bathing machine. It was brought to this cellar and hauled up this central shaft to the rafters. Then it was stored with the rest of the goods in the rooftop run that links all the attics in this street.'

Jenny nodded. She might have guessed that Miles, being such an intelligent boy, was determined to solve the riddle. And she admitted to herself that, give him his due, he had done well.

'I climbed the chimney in the public room at the 'Noah's Ark'. It was difficult but I guess with a little more expertise and the right protective clothing I would soon get the hang of it and scuttle up in no time. But any young person - like yourself, say - could manage it, just, and gain access onto the roof. Then they could hand down the ladder stored there for the smugglers to climb up and pass down the contraband whenever it was needed.

'And no one would know what they were about. In fact, men could even work in broad daylight or when the houses below were being searched. They would be hidden from view by the double hipped roofs and the gully in between them.'

'You have been busy,' Jenny said. She looked at him with

renewed interest. 'And you weren't chased by the skeleton? The one that comes alive when disturbed. The one that lures trespassers to their death.'

'Yes, I was chased. And I admit I was alarmed. But then I've never been fond of cats and I don't appreciate them licking me all over my face. It tickled rather than terrified me,' he fibbed. 'The scallop shells tied around Jinx's neck did, at first, give me quite a shock.'

'And so now you've guessed my own involvement in our midnight trade.'

'I've noticed that washing is no longer there on the line waiting to be dried overnight. It was such a strange assortment of clothes. I guessed it was meant to be a signal. Perhaps for smuggling galleys returning to shore, like 'The Strawberry', for instance.'

There was an awkward silence, which often happens between young friends, but this time Miles was the first to break it. 'Jenny, I don't pretend to fully understand what is going on in this town, and please don't imagine that I agree with it, but for the time being at least, your secret is safe with me.'

Miles was idly running his finger around the rim of his glass. Jenny seized it from his grasp. 'We have a superstition,' she explained, 'that when you do this, a sailor dies. . .'

Then something startling happened. A face appeared at the window. A ghastly, gruesome face lit from below like a ghoul. It leered provocatively. It gave Miles a start and, when she turned around, Jenny, too. Both their hearts beat faster for a moment until they could make sense of the menacing image that bobbed and bounced mid-air amongst the fluttering embers in the whistling wind.

A mask was tied around a pumpkin and held on a stake. The painted pale face displayed exaggerated features - bloated cheeks that indicated sickness and a ruddy nose that denoted drunkenness. The eyes were staring, the nose pinched, and the lips fixed into a sickly smile. The head, which wore a powdered wig with a beribboned queue that waved in the breeze, was attached to a thin body crudely dressed in a crimson jacket, lemon waistcoat and white breeches. All these clothes, however, were tainted and torn so that their former finery was reduced to rags. The arms of the figure were stretched out wide with bunches of straw for hands, like a scarecrow.

This alarming display of a lifeless figure was illuminated in the dusk by fitful glares from lamps, flares and torches. It was accompanied by a tremendous cacophony from an odd assortment of instruments - trumpets, drums, bells, rattles, pots and pans, a fiddle, even a concertina. And its sudden appearance had attracted a huge crowd on the foreshore.

'It's an effigy of William Pitt,' said Jenny's father who had been roused from his slumbers and wandered over to join his daughter and her companion at the window.

'They seem to have got his features right!' observed Miles. 'Look at his golden locks, rouged cheeks and prim nose - all fashioned out of papier mache!'

'Where are they going to display it!' asked Jenny. 'It is a perfect work of art!'

Her father continued, 'They intend burning it in protest outside Walmer Castle. It is their revenge for destroying the luggers. They want us to join them which is why they are waving it at our window. They will soon grow tired - or impatient - and move on,' he assured them. 'Come away from the window and leave them be.'

Jinx was already curled up asleep on his bed when Miles crept back to his attic. He had long since abandoned hope of finding out how the rascally cat made his way in or out of his bedroom. He took the precaution of unscrewing the brass bed nob before it clattered onto the floor and disturbed the cat. Then he too climbed into his bed and tried to sleep.

But he slept not a wink that night. His head was full of strange images that whirled around in a ludicrous gavotte. He was trapped inside a burning lugger. . . he was sinking in a scuttled galley. . . he was chased by an illuminated figure that could only escape by jumping high over the castle battlements. Then he was stuck in a smoking chimney that was closing tightly around his chest. . . so that he could hardly breathe. . . and he knew if he cried out. . . even if he could. . . no one would ever hear him and come to his rescue.

Apart from a grisly, grinning skeleton who leaned its head, opened its jaw and breathed flames of fire.

8

TRIAL

'ALL RISE!' The order came from the Town Sergeant. Everyone stood obediently as the Chief Magistrate, Mayor Powell, entered through a narrow door and took his seat on the raised dais at the front of the courtroom. This was a grand crimson leather padded armchair placed directly under the coat-of-arms of George III and over the bench where his silver mace rested, symbolising his dual authority as Mayor of Deale.

Escorting the Mayor were two further worthies who were acting as supporting magistrates. One was tall and thin with a face the colour of unbaked pastry and who blinked constantly as if extremely short sighted but was, most probably, nervous. The other was a portly country gentleman with a bulbous nose and unruly hair who smiled amenably at the assembly before promptly falling asleep. After a while he slumped so far down into his seat that it was only his strident snoring that reminded everyone, he was still alive.

Miles was reminded of the story of the three little pigs.

The boy had managed to squeeze his way up the winding staircase where townsfolk were standing, hopeful of gaining access into the already packed public gallery. Being small, he was able to fight his way through to the back of that first-floor room where he could hang over the heavily studded wooden gate with carved royal beasts - the lion and the dragon - on stout posts that presented the Cinque Ports arms. From there he would have an unrivalled view of the whole legal proceedings.

The musty courtroom was long and narrow with low beams. The walls were lined with linenfold panelling upon which were displayed dismal portraits of long forgotten dignitaries. Light filtered through the latticed plain glass windows along one side where motes played in the weak, winter sunlight. Candles flickered in brass chandeliers slung from the ceiling but because they were alight early that morning, they only served to add to the pervading gloom.

Spectators were hunched upon the backless benches, facing forwards. To their left was the witness box and to the right, crammed into their own high box, guarded by iron spikes, were the four prisoners. To the far right, built high against the wall, was a double row of seats reserved for twelve jurymen. They remained empty because this was a court of the local petty sessions and not the county quarter sessions which would involve a judge and jury at a full trial.

At intervals, along the courtroom and on the stairs, dragoons were positioned with loaded muskets. Captain Cannons expected to be called first to give evidence and he stood purposely to one side as the charge was read aloud to the confined boatmen. As each of their names were mentioned - John Atkins, Samuel Harris, William Norris, George Rands - these were accompanied by woeful cries from the gallery. 'You are accused of evading taxation on certain goods that you have attempted to import unlawfully into this country,' intoned the big, wigged clerk.

Captain Cannons was indeed called directly, and he took his place confidently in the witness box. He was perfectly prepared to give a precise account of the proceedings late that Saturday night when he had acted upon information from a person or persons unknown. (Miles was relieved that his own name had not been mentioned). He had concealed himself and his men behind one of the luggers beached at the North End. It was approaching midnight when a new built galley, 'The Strawberry', rowed over from Calais, crossed the Downs Anchorage and landed on the beach in the vicinity of Silver Street. His troops surrounded the boat and attempted to arrest the entire crew, four of whom he could with certainty identify as standing opposite him. The remaining two boatmen had escaped and so far, had managed to evade justice.

There was stunned silence after the Captain had made his bold statement. Miles looked around to observe the reaction of the spectators. The courtroom smelled of stale tobacco, damp clothing and unwashed bodies. Folk sprawled against the walls or over the railings. They all appeared despondent because it struck them as inevitable their friends would receive terrible penalties if, as seemed likely, the court accepted the damning account of this prominent military leader. Everyone realised that the law required the boatmen to disprove this evidence rather than that they be assumed innocent until proven guilty.

Mayor Powell adjusted his powdered wig. He put on his spectacles. He took a pinch of snuff. He dusted down his waistcoat with a silk handkerchief. Finally, he leaned over the bench and stared hard at the witness box. Everyone now focused intently upon him. Miles wondered how many of these personal items - silk kerchief, wig powder, scented snuff - were themselves unlawfully imported?

Clearly, it was now the turn of the Chief Magistrate to close question Captain Cannons.

'Was it ever established that any of the boatmen actually owned the galley and therefore also its contents?'

'If the contraband was so cunningly concealed, isn't it possible that the boatmen knew nothing about it themselves?'

'Did they offer any violent resistance to their arrest or did they just flee in the dark, fearful of attack by their unknown assailants?'

These were cleverly worded questions intended to undermine the convincing statement by the Captain of Dragoons. The townsfolk recognised that Mayor Powell, although unpopular for pursuing his own moral crusade, might actually prove to be an ally when the boatmen were, as now, in deep, dire trouble.

The Captain was becoming agitated. He could not disguise his irritation at the constant doubt cast upon his meticulously rehearsed testimony. The whole affair was becoming a travesty. He was about to explode with anger when Mayor Powell quietly suggested:

'Captain Cannons, it might help the court if you could produce at least one independent witness to confirm the incidents you describe on that fateful Saturday night.'

Miles had not expected to be called as a witness! He was still swinging awkwardly on the gate when Captain Cannons, in the foulest temper, strode towards him, his riding boots thundering on the wooden floorboards and resounding throughout the courtroom. He lifted Miles forcibly by the shoulders, carried him protesting along the aisle and deposited him roughly in the witness box. The frightened boy could hardly see above the ledge and almost disappeared from sight.

From this undignified position Miles realised with horror he was next to be questioned by Mayor Powell.

'State your name,' intoned the clerk of the court.

'It is Miles, sir,' the boy whispered, tugging down the front of his torn boating jacket.

'Tell the court precisely what you saw on the beach on Saturday night,' prompted the Captain.

'Captain Cannons, it is, I believe, for me to ask the questions,' corrected the Magistrate. He bent forward to address Miles directly from the bench. 'Tell the court, young man, precisely what you saw on the beach on Saturday night.'

There had been murmurs of disapproval from the spectators when the boy was brought forward struggling. These ceased abruptly the moment he attempted to speak. Miles looked across the broad aisle and stared at the four boatmen who stood with their heads slightly bowed. He noticed there was only the figure of the Town Sergeant separating the prisoners from himself. Understandably, he was hesitant when he attempted his reply.

'If you please, Mr Mayor. . .' he stuttered.

Miles was conscious that his head hardly reached the top of the witness box. The Beadle, sensing his discomfort fetched a leather fire bucket which he turned upside down and bade him stand upon it. This brought Miles in full view of the Magistrate. And the spectators.

'Yes?' prompted the Mayor.

'Yes?' badgered the Captain.

'I was positioned behind one of the luggers. 'Primrose'. I read her name clearly. She was beached opposite the slops shop. The Captain was there with his dragoons, about thirty of them, and they were hiding too. . .'

Miles sensed he had now the attention of everyone and he grew bolder in his demeanour.

'It was very quiet. You could only hear the wind and the waves. Suddenly, 'The Strawberry' came into sight. She was being rowed by about half a dozen men. She hit the shingle with a mighty crunch. The men jumped out and looked around. . . I think for support. . . but no one came so they carried the boat up to the top of the beach.'

'And you saw all this form where you were concealed?' asked the Mayor.

'The Captain gave a signal. He raised his arm sharply. His troops surrounded the galley. The crew were taken by surprise. There was a struggle. A few boatmen were able to slip away but the troops chased after them. I think it was only because the men know the alleys so well, they managed to escape.' Miles faltered, 'But that is only my opinion. . .

'And are you able to recognise any of these boatmen, the ones that evaded the dragoons on Saturday night? Look around the courtroom and tell me if you see any of the crew here today.' The Mayor took off his spectacles and placed them on the ledger before him. 'Take your time.'

The Mayor, the Captain, the Beadle, the bewigged clerk, the spectators and all four boatmen looked expectantly at Miles who was cowering in the witness box. He knew that the Captain wanted him to point out the culprits, but he also guessed that the Mayor would be just as pleased if he did not. There was an air of expectancy as Miles turned towards the crowd. He was in no doubt that much depended upon his answer.

He had never before in his life been faced with such a dilemma. He realised for the first time how difficult it is to identify a person for the second time around. That night the crew were stressed and angry but now their faces were in comparative repose. He was almost certain he recognised a couple of men among the spectators from that dramatic night apart from those four standing opposites him in the dock. He was deeply troubled that he held their fate in his hands.

He found, though, he could easily interpret the expressions of the men and women in the courtroom who waited for his decisive answer. They showed fear. . . anxiety. . . distress. . . alarm. Forever afterwards he would blame himself for what he thought was his own cowardice. He was about to avoid the intense pressure placed upon him by responsible adults for those few moments in the crowded courtroom.

Miles was barely audible when he lifted his head and spoke directly to the Mayor.

'It was a dark night. Everything happened at once. It was late and I was sleepy. In truth, I could never be certain. . .'

Miles dared not wait for Mayor Powell to deliver his judgement. When he had been dismissed as a witness - and an unreliable one at that - he pushed his way, ashamed and embarrassed, through the stuffy courtroom. He raced down the steps unable to restrain the tears of frustration that blinded his view. Once free, he ran for all his might, towards the seafront but found even the side streets were packed solid with furious inhabitants.

He stopped only when he reached the foreshore. There he leaned against an upright cannon acting as a street bollard to catch his breath. He looked over his shoulder towards the slops shop but there was no sign of Jenny nor her father. When he left London, less than a fortnight ago, he could not have envisaged the dramas that had enfolded so rapidly in this little seaport. He no longer knew who to turn to for friendship or advice, nor even whom he dared trust.

More and more people were spilling onto the beach. Soon an unruly crowd assembled. Everyone was becoming wildly animated. Miles caught snatches of conversation that sounded ominous. Words and phrases were carried along by the wind: 'Guilty!'. . . 'Transportation'. . . 'Botany Bay.' Evidently, the Mayor had been obliged to bestow a terrible punishment that would inevitably destroy the lives of so many boatmen's families.

Miles realised, by now, that one fact could not be disputed. 'The Strawberry' had more than four oars. This was illegal since the galley could have no other purpose than to evade the revenue cutters when in the act of smuggling. It would be sawn into three never again to venture across the English Channel. Her crew, however, had been helped by Mayor Powell in some small measure. He had established that they had not offered violent resistance to their arrest. They had therefore been awarded a less severe penalty than the proscribed death sentence.

Now the significance of that featureless black hull, lacking masts and sails, permanently moored four or five miles distant in the Downs Anchorage, became suddenly all too clear. This was a redundant frigate that had been converted by the Admiralty into a prison hulk, a leaking, stinking vessel that was unfit for human habitation. Convicted criminals - male, female and even children - were imprisoned there temporarily in overcrowded conditions while awaiting their transportation to penal colonies in the New World.

As Miles watched, a black flag was hoisted atop a tall pole along the coast and a gun was fired in acknowledgement from the looming hulk. Even before the smoke had cleared from that single mighty boom a long galley was carefully lowered down its port side. A marine became discernible sitting bolt upright in the stern and a crew of eight broken, miserable men - convicts themselves - began to row reluctantly, rhythmically towards the shore.

From his vantage point Miles watched the head of the slow, solemn procession now wending its way from the Court Hall via Middle Street and Silver Street towards the seafront. Captain Cannons, mounted on his chestnut horse, stared straight ahead, as he led his men triumphantly, his sabre held aloft. Four mounted troops followed, riding two abreast, at a steady trot. Behind, and Miles could only just glimpse this through the jostling crowd, shuffled the four boatmen convicted of smuggling, manacled in pairs, striving to keep pace while maintaining their dignity. Bringing up the rear was another body of mounted troops, although Miles could not tell how many there were since they were barely visible above the heads of the bitterly resentful townsfolk.

The fate of the boatmen was evident to everyone watching. Miles felt a great wave of sadness pass over him as he prepared to witness the dismal sight of the ferrying of shackled convicts out to their floating, rotting prison. The scene reminded him of wild animals herded - two by two - into a crowded Noah's Ark.

Then pandemonium erupted. What happened next was a concerted and audacious attack on the mounted escort. Ropes trailing across the street had been concealed by straw purposely strewn on the cobbles. Their knotted ends were held by boatmen leaning out of their first-floor windows. On a given signal they were pulled tight. The result was that the rear guard of dragoons was hopelessly entangled by the taut ropes. These troops were ensnared at chest height and were unable to reach for their swords as they struggled to control their rearing horses.

At the top of Beach Street angry crowds closed in on the leading dragoons. Boatmen tugged at the horses' reigns and knocked over their riders with blows from stakes found scorched and scattered on the beach after the burning of their luggers and galleys. At the same time women and children along Silver Street lobbed an assortment of makeshift weapons: kettles, saucepans, milking stools, coal scuttles, chamber pots, even that tuneless concertina from the inn. It was a concerted effort that expressed the anger of an entire boating community for the loss of their prized beach craft.

Captain Cannons and his troops were taken unawares. They were totally unprepared for the ferocity of this pitched street battle. The noise was deafening. Shouts and screams. . . curses and jeers. . . cries and neighs. The Captain was furious with the crowd and with his ineffectual escort. He lashed out in all directions while being pushed and shoved and goaded himself. All to no avail. For in the violent melee his prisoners had inexplicably disappeared. They had simply vanished into thin salt sea air.

Miles' attention was caught by an innocuous horse drawn covered wagon making its solitary way in the opposite direction to the ambuscade. Captain Cannons, ever observant, noticed it too and abandoned his assault upon the crowd to give chase.

Hunters are notoriously sure footed. . . but then horses and pebbles are not compatible. When the Captain attempted to break into a gallop, his mount lost her footing among the charred timbers and tarred pebbles of that steep, ridged beach. When he spurred her onwards, she stumbled and shied? The Captain lost control, slipped from his saddle and tumbled onto the shingle to the derision of the crowd.

Slow and purposeful, meanwhile, Thomas Oakley's delivery wagon headed towards the spanking new windmill at the North End of Deale.

Jenny must have been the only person in Deale who did not know of the escape of the four prisoners. That was because she was at that time making her way along the Ancient Highway to the neighbouring town of Sandwich. She carried a heavy wicker basket generously packed with tempting delicacies and covered with a cheery red speckled cloth. Her purpose was to visit a highly regarded gentleman who had recently fallen on hard times.

She crossed the little humped bridge over the Stour and skirted the town by the Quay.

Then she turned left by the Tudor Barbican and walked through the twisting, turning medieval streets - convoluted as a spider's web - with their quaint, half timbered, jettied houses. She might have paused to admire their carved doorways, high gables, latticed windows and brick chimneys protruding through tiled roofs. Instead, she concentrated on locating the concealed entrance to a concealed passage leading to the town gaol.

Holy Ghost Alley twisted and turned more times than a cockerel on a weathervane in a wintry gale. Bulging walls were built of stone and brick and knapped flint. Jenny squeezed her way through narrowest part of the passage formed from bulging wattle and daub walls of an ancient house before she arrived opposite St. Peter's Church.

At last, Jenny was facing the town gaol that occupied one corner of the walled churchyard. It was a formidable brick building rendered white with a studded door set into a timber archway. She tugged a rope and a bell jangled in the distance bringing a lazy response from the turnkey. He obliged by letting her into the cobbled passage, first examining the contents of her basket and helping himself to a leg of chicken, before opening the iron grille of the single cell to her right.

The cell was light enough but cold and damp. There was a paved floor strewn with stale straw and a high window protected by thick bars. Along one wall was a stone slab that served at once as a table, a chair and a bedstead. There was neither furniture, bedding nor washing facilities. The succession of occupants had been made to suffer hardship even before their impending trial.

Alone on the cold, hard bed there sat, with his head in his hands, that once respected coachman, Josiah Goggins. How had the mighty fallen! For warmth he still wore his hat, his muffler and his greatcoat where, in the buttonhole, a posy wilted, like his love for the young serving girl at the coffee shop. He looked up at his visitor with tears in his eyes and his face expressed both remorse and shame. He repeatedly whispered: 'Nancy . . . Nancy . . . Oh, Nancy.' Over and over again.

Jenny sat down beside him and made soothing noises as she

took his hand and dried his eyes with her own silk kerchief.

'It is good of you to come,' sniffed Mr Goggins.

She laid the bright cloth between them on the stone slab and produced plates and mugs but no knives or forks for an indoor picnic. From her basket she took out a hunk of bread, a cold meat pie, cheese, fruit and even a small stone bottle of ale but, alas, no chicken. She tempted Mr Goggins to try a little of everything but did not persist when he said he was too distressed to eat anything. Instead of fussing she gently suggested he might like to help himself to 'a little something perhaps a little later'.

Mr Goggins wanted to present his own version of his story to his kind visitor. He explained how, purely as a favour, he had loaded his coach with parcels for his sweetheart's brother in Canterbury. Unknown to him, the parcels contained dress materials on which the import tax had not been paid. They were intended to be resold, he understood now perfectly, for top prices in the London markets.

When his post coach had been stopped as he entered the town gates he was just as surprised as the Revenue Men to find the parcels - and there were a lot of them - contained contraband. It was a complete mystery to him where they came from apart from the fact that he was acting as a favour in delivering them for his sweetheart. He had no idea (sob) no idea at all (sob, sob) of the origin of their contents, he swore (a big sob) 'upon his very life'.

Jenny was not entirely convinced by Mr Goggins' story. But she remained kind and tactful. She was familiar with the serving girl at 'The Three Mariners' who had professed her undying love to this gullible, elderly gentleman. Privately she considered her to be nothing more than 'a perfect little minx'. At the same time, a common maid would hardly have been able to afford to acquire, let alone purchase, such expensive materials. Surely, it would have been obvious to all and sundry that they had been smuggled? Mr Goggins had been tricked, that seemed certain, into handling the bulky parcels and their illegal contents. But it was extremely difficult for her to credit the coachman's complete innocence in the matter. 'Love,' they say, 'is truly blind.'

Whether she believed the whole of Mr Goggins story or not, Jenny was sensitive enough to realise that at that moment he needed, more than anything, a true friend to console him. The truth of the matter, she decided, would be for the law courts to judge. Right now, Jenny was prepared simply to be that comforting companion.

She lingered a little longer before she attempted her long walk home. As she left, she reached into a corner of her basket and brought out her own nosegay of sweet herbs which she kissed before popping into Mr Goggins' top buttonhole.

Mr Goggins smiled through his tears and reflected how kind Jenny had been to him. 'Not all young people were spoiled and selfish,' he considered. Jenny, for one, was generous and gracious and she was already in his misty eyes a fine young lady.

'Mind where you go, laddie. This is not a playground! Find somewhere else to idle away your time!'

Miles had wandered aimlessly, southwards along the beach towards the stunted wooden jetty that stretched only a short distance out to sea. Beyond lay the Navy Yard with its stout timber gates and high boundary wall that prohibited unauthorised access. Here, where Miles paused, was the Customs boathouse, a substantial red brick building standing proud atop the foreshore. It had immense double doors, flung wide open, although guarded, from which several straggling lines of greased skids led down to the water's edge. Its distinctive feature, however, was an ornate Dutch gable, that often appeared on important houses and buildings in the town of Deale.

After the traumas of the last two days, Miles felt he need a little time to himself. He wanted to gather his thoughts which were becoming confused with conflicting ideas of right and wrong. He was unsure, for instance, just where his sympathies lay, and he was particularly distressed that violence had erupted so quickly, particularly among the boating fraternity among which he had made many friends.

As he stumbled along the beach, he was careful to dodge the piles of blackened timber from the burned luggers and galleys that were still smouldering. He reflected in his young mind that this harsh retribution could only have an adverse effect on a hard-working community.

While he contemplated this situation, he paused to kick shells dumped on a cockleswamp but they were no substitute for a football and he succeeded only in stubbing his foot. The stench, in any case, repulsed him so he meandered onwards. It pervaded even the usual beach smells of rope, varnish, tar and fish.

The sea was calm now and the waves lapped gently but there was an absence of boats, birds, seals and anything of interest on the water. He was, however, drawn to the small craft that were winched high up the shingle in front of the open doors of the boathouse.

The voice that addressed him sharply came from a little man who sat on a wooden crate smoking a clay pipe. He had a ruddy face and a profusion of ginger whiskers. He wore a tired sailor's jacket over a tatty brown smock and a shapeless leather hat. This kept the wood shavings out of his unruly red hair for this short-tempered man was formerly a ship's carpenter, now employed exclusively by the Customs. A canvas bag with rope handles lay open beside him and a variety of tools spilled out onto the pebbles.

Miles was in no mood to make enemies, so he apologised and turned to walk back along the beach. His educated voice and polite manner impressed the carpenter who instantly adjusted his view of a poorly dressed boatmen's boy and he decided to engage him in conversation. He scooped up his tool bag and strolled over to one of the beached boats. He examined its structure with his steady eyes and ran his rough hands along one side of the hull.

'Laddie, I was a bit short. Stay awhile if you will. You can talk to me as I work.'

Miles, who detected a fragrance of sawdust, warmed to the fiery carpenter and soon found that he was in good company after all.

'Cap'n Crow, at your service,' he announced and offered Miles his chubby hand.

'Hand me my mallet. I am about to replace this top plank which has split in several places. The planks are not attached to any frame. The hull is built up by overlapping planks. This gives the hull greater flexibility. It is far more able to take the strain of rough waves. All Deale boats are 'clinker' built.' He tapped the hull, almost lovingly. 'She is a fine specimen, now, is 'Violet'.'

The carpenter hammered at the splintered plank between these most informative short sentences. Then he tugged at the nails until he had prized it away. Miles appreciated being allowed to watch this man at work. He was always fascinated by experts, whatever their field. Here was a man with a lifetime's experience of sailing ships and beach craft.

In the space of a few minutes Miles' new acquaintance had regaled him with tales of hairbreadth escapes from pirates. . . wrecks by storms. . . seasickness. . . rats. . . fleas . . . scurvy. . . the violent lurching and rolling of a fully rigged vessel with the passengers tumbling all over the swaying top deck. . . crews packed in close confinement in dark, dingy cabins. . . shifting sails. . . foul water. . . warm, flat beer. . . bread breeding worms and biscuits hard as pebbles on the foreshore.

He hardly paused for breath! But when he did, Miles was determined to show that he had acquired a little nautical knowledge since his time on the Kent coast. He pointed to the craft under repair. 'Is this a galley?' The carpenter looked at him, clearly impressed.

'You are almost correct, laddie. This is a galley punt. She is faster and lighter than a galley and is even more seaworthy. She is meant to be sailed although, of course, she can also be rowed. But not at the same time! There are four rowing thwarts - there you see - and she can be steered by oar as well as rudder when she's under sail.'

Sensing he had a captive audience, the carpenter continued to educate his young friend.

'The mast is light enough to assemble when it is breezy and just as easy to ship when it becomes calm again. But she needs to carry a lot of ballast - that's because her draught is extremely shallow - and this needs to be shifted to the weather side whenever the crew tack. It's a tiresome business and extremely hard work, whether rowing or sailing across this wild road, known the world over as the Downs!'

Miles was proud to think that he had fairly followed this detailed explanation of complicated maritime matters.

Captain Crow began replacing the plank with shaped timber which he had already cut precisely to size. Miles was required to hold one end until it fitted exactly over the one below. Then he resumed hammering, but he still spoke - breathlessly - between blows.

'The boatmen call them 'knock-toes'. That, before you ask, is because when there is a full complement of crew - three or four men - they are so cramped once inside they all tend to knock their toes together!'

Miles leant against the low hull and looked over the top and into the boat. 'It does seem to be very narrow. . . but deep. . . and open. I guess the crew get very wet?'

'Aye, that they do! But they get used to it! Or so I'm led to believe. The boatmen mainly use them for piloting. These boats, mind - those that belong to the Customs - are employed for retrieving contraband, carrying provisions and, on occasions, lifesaving.'

'Contraband?'

'Ah, that's got you attention, laddie. You cannot surely have failed to have heard that Deale is notorious for its smuggling activities.' Miles had, indeed, but he knew far more than he was prepared to admit. He hoped his expression gave nothing away.

There was no need for him to worry, however, as the carpenter had turned his full attention to mending the galley punt. He was tapping the top with his mallet, making sure it was true, and making minor adjustments. Then he patted the replacement plank with satisfaction before gathering up his tools and stowing them in his canvas workbag.

'As you're originally from London, I guess, laddie, your head will be full of romantic tales of smuggling? You can forget that notion, I can tell you. Men will protect their ill-gotten gains at any cost. Innocent folk have been hurt, and let's not deny it, killed. Smuggling is a violent business, to be sure, as you may have observed today.'

'And on both sides. . .' qualified Miles.

The carpenter paused and stared at the boy. 'Aye, yes, that I won't deny. You learn fast.'

The carpenter retrieved his pipe and pointed with it towards the enormous boathouse. 'There are several more boats stored in there - a couple of luggers and two or three galleys. You are welcome to take a peep but don't wander inside. Several of the smaller craft were confiscated from convicted smugglers and are now turned against them, to catch them in the act!' He chortled at his own fancies and smiled warmly at Miles.

'Don't the galleys have to be cut into three if they have been caught with contraband?' asked Miles. 'Isn't that a waste?'

'Not entirely. The boatmen are nothing if not resourceful. They turn them into homes. And very comfortable ones too. You may have seen a fine example not far from here.'

'Yes, I have. It belongs to Queenie. It was built by her hubby, a 'chippy', just like you.'

'Not quite like me! I stayed the right side of the law. Queenie's husband drowned while he was being pursued by the Customs. There was a reward put out for his capture and he attempted to flee to France. He was heading towards the North Goodwin when his galley was holed by a wreck. It was low tide, so he made a break for the highest point that dries in the sun, that part sailors call 'Jamaica Island'. Lord knows why!

'When the tide rose, he waved his shirt at passing ships, but the crews assumed he was skylarking and sailed on. He'd never learned to swim, you see, which is why he drowned.' The carpenter shook his head in despair at such a futile loss of a man's life.

'His galley was recovered and towed ashore by the Customs. But it was beyond repair and of little use for their own fleet. Instead, his widow was allowed to keep it and so, you see, it was Queenie, herself, who converted it into a cosy seaside home.'

Miles was further confused by hearing an alternative tale of Queenie's beloved 'ubby's demise. He could quite easily discern; however, which story was more likely to be true.

He wondered, too, whether her boathouse might be the ideal place for a smuggling ring to gather unobserved. Silver, the parrot, had repeated something he had heard there about 'The Strawberry' sailing across from France. And he had seen that fragment from a poster offering a reward which might have referred to Queenie's 'ubby' or just as likely another member of the local smuggling fraternity.

All the same, he could think of nothing to add on this subject, so he decided to pose another question instead. 'Can it really be that wrong to smuggle? Surely, it does little harm once in a while. People are entitled to a little luxury, now and then.'

'Now who, I wonder, has filled your head with such utter nonsense?' The carpenter's mood had changed abruptly. 'Smuggling is not a few boatmen dabbling in illicit affairs. It is big business with huge gains. This whole town is built on the 'Wicked Trade'. And it ought to be stamped out!'

Miles wished he had not broached the subject but had the good sense to hold his tongue. The carpenter was definitely agitated, and his face reddened alarmingly. He waved his pipe around in the air almost as if it was become a weapon in his hand.

'Mr Pitt has imposed fair taxes on luxury goods only. The people who want these items can easily afford to pay the taxes on them. The money raised helps to fund the war effort. And if you care to look in that direction,' the carpenter indicated with his pipe, 'you will see that France is not such a great distance from our shores.' Miles did look and agreed this fact could not be denied.

'Now you can help me run this craft up the beach and into the boatshed, my fine young feller? All boats along this coast ought, by law, to be hidden. Just in case the enemy try to steal them for their own devilish aims.'

Miles rolled up his sleeves and turned his back to help edge the repaired craft up and over the high ridge of shingle.

'And if they should decide to invade - and I think that more than likely - then, you, laddie, and your family, will be the first to demand protection from those rascally Frenchies.'

9

WINDMILL

A T THE FIRST stroke of midnight from the church clock, Miles slipped silently out of bed. He had been careful to remove the brass bed nob that might fall onto the floor and alert the residents that he was wide awake. He had popped it into the pocket of his greatcoat slung over his borrowed blanket to give him extra warmth at night. Then he crept down the two flights of stairs, along the dark passage and into the kitchen at the rear.

The fire was settling in the iron grate although its heat still stung his bare knees as he crept past in his stockinged feet. Its glowing coals in the absence of candlelight steered him towards the larder door in one corner. For a moment he jumped - and almost cried out aloud - as his head bumped against a jugged hare hanging on a steel hook by its hind feet.

Feeling his way along the high marble shelves he located a substantial pork pie, identified by its crinkly crust, a meaty mutton bone and a round of cheese. Deftly, he placed these foods into his square kerchief which he tied with a firm knot. As he retraced his steps, he was conscious of the thumping of the Parliamentary clock in the public bar. Why does the ticking of a clock always seem much louder and faster in the middle of the night? Back in his attic, Miles snatched some guilt-ridden sleep in the still, small hours.

Long before the inn became alive, Miles awoke once more, dressed and let himself out of the inn door. Aunt Gwen had trained her servants well and they would be up to light the kitchen fire at the crack of dawn. He was becoming accustomed, not only to his early start to each day, but his freedom to wander as he pleased. No one seemed to question, let alone care, about his solitary activities. It would be hard for him to adjust to the strict routine of his sheltered family life once he returned to London.

He held the flap of his greatcoat collar across his chin with one hand and with the other supported the awkward bulge which was the stolen food tucked around his waist. He had forgotten to discard that brass bed nob from the deep pocket, and this now bumped annoyingly against his leg. He did appear a strange sight! Except that no one could take a good look at him because it was such a damp, rimy morning. He was part concealed from view by the morning haze as he made his furtive way towards the seafront.

He could hear the distant clattering and clanking of tools accompanied by words of advice, encouragement and occasional reprimand from workmen. They were attempting to salvage the burnt-out husks of their luggers and galleys. Already, they had made sterling progress in rendering a couple of them seaworthy. To Miles, though, it had seemed a hopeless task. But then he had not counted upon the resilience and determination of boatmen who were readily sharing their skills and labour. It was far too expensive for them to secure the services of professional boatbuilders. There was a remarkable community spirit among the North Enders.

Miles picked his way with trepidation along the damp pebbles. His foot might slip on the greased skids; his head could knock on the spars of the charred luggers. He might stumble into one of the wooden capstans or trips on the projecting steps of the boatmen's huts. Worse still, there was a chance he might drop the tell-tale bundle of food that he had purloined from the pantry of the 'Noah's Ark'.

Scurrying northwards, Miles found himself disorientated by the cloying mist which distorted all the familiar landmarks. The bathing huts, for instance, hovered overhead, their slender iron wheels almost imperceptible. Beyond, Queenie's boathouse, too, seemed suspended in mid-air, the greyness blurring the defining line between sea and sky. Ahead, the landward stone bastion of the ancient castle halted his further progress along the beach towards the Sandhills. Above, loomed the slender white smock windmill rising like a phantom, its distinctive boat cap invisible and just the tip of one skeletal sail discernible, reaching almost to the ground.

He had arrived at his secret destination.

The mill was dormant. There was a complete absence of wind. Its sails were stationary. Yet outside there was a flurry of activity. Miller Oakley was loading heavy flour sacks onto the back of the covered delivery wagon. Jenny was leading the hardy young workhorse to the front and attaching its harness. Miles slipped past them, shrouded still in dense mist, and sneaked inside the mill with his bulky bundle through the propped open door in its low brick base.

Unfamiliar with the geography of a working windmill, Miles allowed himself to be guided by the flights of steps and positioning of ladders. These would direct him in turn to each successive floor. So... quickly across the dark, cluttered ground floor where the fresh sacks of flour were stored to the wide, worn steps leading to the stone floor. There were two pairs of grindstones, idle at present, so the mill was unnaturally quiet. Miles wove his way around them fearing that his footsteps would be heard as he crossed this first floor to the next set of sturdy steps.

Mice scuttled across the bowed floorboards unaware that they were being observed by a plump, ginger, tom cat, watching intently from one of the rafters. An acrobatic spider swung spectacularly on its delicate silk thread across a cracked, cobwebbed window.

This second floor was where the coarse grain was stored in hessian sacks waiting to be fed into the square bins that began the process of milling. These bins were situated above the great spur wheel that laboriously turned the heavy pair of millstones one floor below. The dry grain smelled musty, and the air was heavy with dust as Miles picked his way past the low sides of the huge bins and tiptoed towards the long ladder in the corner alongside the iron chain hoist connecting with the boat cap.

Miles could hear footsteps on the heavy boards above his head and rough voices that told him that the escaped boatmen were camping there even before he climbed the ladder and peered inside the interior of the windmills' cap. The four men stopped in their tracks, caught unawares, and dismayed to find that their hiding place had been discovered by a mere boy.

Miles stood on the middle rung with his head level with the floorboards. He reached down to his waist and retrieved the bundle which he placed in front of him. Balancing precariously, he untied the kerchief and edged the food parcel across the floor. The men stared at it momentarily before bursting into laughter. One of them then grabbed him by the shoulders and gently lifted him into the mill's spacious cap.

The boy stood and looked around him. There was far more space than he expected because there was plenty of height for the men to stand. The wooden cogs of the giant brake wheel that turned the machinery was raised a few feet above their heads. Even had it been revolving they would still have been perfectly safe. There would have been no need for them to duck. Yet this was still a confined space in which to confine four burly boatmen. Desperately, each man craved his liberty.

The men tucked into their welcome breakfast. Miles assumed there would be no shortage of bread in a windmill, but he regretted he had brought them nothing to drink from the inn. There was a limit to what he could carry or conceal. As they shared their meal, they tousled his hair and patted him on the back. They made jovial comments although thankfully no one referred to his feeble performance at the Court House.

All the same, they wanted to know how he had tracked them down. They were surprised by his simple answer. Miles told them how he had watched as Oakley's wagon rode away from the affray. He had guessed that they were stowed inside and were heading for the windmill.

Suddenly, the mill began to shake. Gently, at first, but it was a definite movement. There were no windows in the boat cap, but the men realised that this meant that the wind was strengthening. This would disperse the mist and allow Thomas Oakley to resume milling.

The conical structure of the mill acted as a funnel for sound.

The higher up the more distinct it became as it travelled. Above the wind, the men could hear something far more alarming. They paused from their munching and crunching to listen. It was the pounding of horses' hoofs. A party of dragoons was thundering rapidly towards Sandown windmill.

Incredibly, there were half a dozen windmills in the immediate vicinity of Deale. This high number - only two other north Kent towns had more - was explained by the fact that troops were beginning to assemble on the south east coast in anticipation of a prolonged war with France. Quartermasters commissioned merchant millers to supply flour for the numerous military camps recently established in the immediate district. Consequently, the price of corn for civilians rose sharply and its spiralling cost caused them considerable hardship.

Unscrupulous millers took the opportunity for brisk trading. They formed a syndicate in order to sell their services at extortionate prices - far higher even than the London markets - and although concerned clergymen and disgusted dignitaries complained bitterly, they were powerless to act.

Labourers, locally, went hungry.

Thomas Oakley became their champion. A former highly respected Mayor of Deale, Oakley was also a brewer, banker and a shipping agent for the Dutch East Company. He vowed to break the cartel of the greedy millers by constructing his own windmill in order to trade at competitive prices. His idea was that the inhabitants of North Deale would become self-sufficient which would ensure that rival owners would be forced to abandon their nefarious practices. After all, he observed, there was no shortage of cornfields in the surrounding countryside.

He acquired a level patch of land at the extreme north of the town to erect his proposed windmill adjacent to Sandown Castle. This was the perfect location since not only did it catch the wind when mills inland fell short, but it was visible to captains of ships when entering or leaving the Downs. They were compelled to send ashore for supplies - flour for fresh bread when becalmed at anchor or hard biscuits in preparation for a sea voyage - and Sandown was, by far, the most convenient mill for them to trade. The only problem with his choice was that the garrison of the castle had commandeered his new mill house, built long and low to avoid obstructing the free flow of the prevailing winds, as a temporary canteen!

Thomas Oakley employed local craftsmen for the building of his coastal windmill. A small army of skilled labourers - bricklayers, carpenters, stone dressers, sail makers - worked indefatigably over a matter of several weeks. Boatbuilders were adept at supplying the timber cladding for the smock since their skills were identical for the construction of their own luggers and galleys. Finally, the structure was painted stark white to ensure that it could be observed from a great distance by Royal or Merchant Navy ships entering the Downs Anchorage.

Daily, Miller Oakley stood and watched the progress of his windmill with immense pride. His slender smock mill stood on a low brick base and rose over two floors. It terminated in an immense Kentish boat cap with a revolving fantail that would keep the four sails constantly in the eye of the wind. This would, all millwrights knew, prevent the whole structure from toppling! There would be no first-floor stage because the four sails would run close to the ground. He had chosen the perfect location. Sandown Windmill was prominently placed to draw its motive power in an easterly wind directly from the sea.

Once completed, Thomas Oakley, generous to a fault, invited all his workmen, their wives and children to a 'topping out' ceremony. Trestle tables were laden with freshly baked bread, cured meats and strong cheeses, while home brewed beer, ale and cider was poured liberally from heavy wooden casks.

Families danced to the lively accompaniment provided by the fiddler from the 'Noah's Ark'. John Hubbard jigged a hornpipe, although he had never been to sea, while Granny Penance sang romantic ballads, although she had never been in love. There was lots of noise but little tune. By then, nobody cared, as they were light-hearted and lightheaded with eating, drinking and abundant merrymaking.

To everyone's amusement - but Miller Oakley's consternation - his daredevil son, Tom, presently employed as his father's apprentice, scaled the heights of the new windmill. He carried a union flag in his teeth and then secured it to the summit where it fluttered gayly in the breeze! Triumphantly, he then balanced on his head atop the boat cap!

At the end of the celebrations, Miller Oakley set the sails - garlanded with patriotic red, white and blue pennants - in motion to indicate that Sandown Mill was 'open for business.' Everyone cheered as the decorated sails idled round in a moderate coastal breeze.

From this day onwards this would be the new mill's proud motto: 'Flour to the People!'

A hand reached out and grabbed Miles by the ankle from the

open hatch. Alarmed, he turned and looked down. There stood his former friend, Captain Cannons, his face crimson with fury. Although he struggled violently, Miles could not extricate himself from the iron grasp of his clenched fist.

In one spilt second it occurred to Miles that he had been the means of leading the dragoons to the fugitives' hiding place in the windmill's cap.

Miles struggled to keep his balance. He was held fast by one leg. He kicked backwards with the other. But to little purpose. The Captain began to pull him relentlessly towards him. There was a danger he would fall down the hatch.

Twist. . . turn. . . kick. . . spit. . . Miles was like a scalded cat!

Suddenly, he remembered the brass bed nob in his greatcoat pocket. He reached deep inside to retrieve it. Then he twisted his body round and bowled it like a cricket ball at Captain Cannon's forehead. At such short range it made its mark. The impact knocked the surprised dragoon down the narrow ladder. He fell backwards with an unrepeatable curse!

Instantly, the boatmen reacted. They ran over to the sack hoist and shinned down its long iron chain. Former sailors, they were accustomed to descending ropes at speed and in motion in answer to the bo'sun's shrill whistle! They made a rapid descent to the bin floor.

The last one - John Atkins - picked Miles up by the waist and lifted him safely out of harm's way on top of the great horizontal toothed wheel, the 'wallower'.

As the boatmen made for the flight of steps down to the stone floor, they were met by the dragoons climbing - one by one - in their heavy riding boots upwards towards the grain store. Dragoons and boatmen now confronted each other and prepared to fight alongside the low panels of the grain bins. The dragoons were armed with swords and pistols although they were reluctant to fire from close quarters at unarmed men.

But the boatmen were resourceful, and they soon armed themselves. They picked up the half empty sacks of grain and employed them as makeshift sandbags. This proved to be far more effective than clubs or cudgels in the confined space of the bin floor.

One boatman - Will Norris - placed himself at the top of the steps and repeatedly walloped a heavy sack over each unsuspecting dragoon as his head popped above the open hatch.

Another - Sam Harris - managed to stun a dragoon who promptly slipped on the loose grain with his heavy boots and fell headfirst down the wide chute. Momentarily, he was stuck fast with his legs kicking in the air before being pulled free by a comrade.

Two other men - George Rands and John Atkins - fought mercilessly with their improvised weapons. The hessian sacks split. . . the dust flew. . . and the men coughed and choked and snuffled and spluttered. Everyone struggled to breathe.

Here was THE most spectacular pillow fight!

Meanwhile Captain Cannons had partially recovered and, nursing his forehead, retraced his steps to the boat cap in pursuit of Miles. He looked all around. Miles had vanished!

Then it occurred to him to look up and he saw Miles perched on the huge timber wallower. Squatting there, the boy was way beyond reach.

The Captain noticed the miller's ladder propped against the far wall but in the short time he took to position it, Miles had scampered across the windshaft to the vertical brake wheel. He eased his way through the timber spokes and out through the narrow hatch in the side of the boat cap. He had no idea where this might lead but his only aim was to escape from the furious Captain of Dragoons.

The hatch opened just above the crosstree that carried the windmill's four robust sails. Miles did not stop to think. In any case, there was no turning back. He stretched out and grabbed one of the stationary sails. He pulled himself out into the open, slithering on his tummy, then swung round until he could gain a foothold on one of the wide sail bars. His plan now was to climb down using the sail as a giant ladder. He knew this might end in mid-air - the mist was thinning but it still obscured the length of the sail - and after that he would simply have to pluck up courage and drop to the ground.

Captain Cannons, by now, had climbed the ladder, mounted the wallower and stepped over to a wooden ledge. There was no way that he could follow Miles through the narrow hatch, but he was determined that he would not lose track of his agile, artful, athletic quarry. Employing both his hands and his burly shoulder, he lifted the stout wooden bar that acted as the sail brake. Callously, he waited for the inevitable effect of his reckless action, the consequences of which he could most certainly guess.

The four slender sails stuttered and stalled before they started to spin clockwise, driven by the sporadic gusts of wind. The fantail droned endlessly as it began to turn the boat cap almost imperceptibly in order to correct the position of the sails. Alarmingly, the wooden floorboards throbbed as the milling apparatus sprang into life. The lumbering wallower moaned and groaned as it revolved to engage the wheels on each of the two floors below.

There was a tremendous cacophony caused by the rattling and rumbling of the mighty spur wheel, the grating and grinding of the underdrift stones and the clinking and clanking of bells below giving timely warning that the hoppers were dangerously running on empty.

Soldiers and sailors stopped in their tracks. They were totally disorientated by the conflicting sounds of the machinery as its components engaged and the confusing movement from the sails as their shadows swept hypnotically across the vibrating floor.

They were left in little doubt that a working windmill was an extremely hazardous place.

Outside, the reluctant stowaway was swung repeatedly round while clinging desperately two thirds down one of the shutters. Outwards and onwards and upwards. He bit his lip. . . he gritted his teeth. . . his eyes nearly popped out of his head! His coat flared out and his cap shot off. Round and round he went at a swift pace on this giant Catherine wheel. Each half turn he was left hanging upside down. Constantly, he cried out in alarm. But there was no one at hand who could possibly rescue him.

He couldn't climb up. He couldn't climb down. His hands and feet held fast. He lost all sense of direction. He felt giddy and dizzy as the blood rushed to his head. Then the inevitable happened. He lost his grip, and he flew through the air. Afterwards, he could never recall whether he jumped or whether he fell.

'Aagh. . . aagh. . .
aagh. . . AAGH!'

He floated for what seemed like an age but was really only a few seconds. His arms and legs thrashed and flailed. Then he landed with a dull, comforting thud onto the canvas cover of the delivery wagon. Startled, he could not believe his good fortune. But he hardly had time to gather his thoughts when he heard a decisive command: 'Gee up!'

Jenny was driving the wagon away at speed with Miles still splayed out on its spacious top until they were both swallowed up by that gently, rolling sea mist.

Miles lay on his back staring up at the motley sky. He was still recovering from his aerial acrobatics. For a while pom pom clouds still juggled above him. The wintry sun bounced around as if at a fairground. Seagulls whizzed across his vision as if shot from a cannon in a circus. Gradually everything returned to its allotted place and resumed its natural order. But without any appreciative applause.

'The still before the storm,' announced Jenny. She, too, was watching the milky white clouds as they raced across the tortoiseshell sky. She sat cross-legged opposite Miles in a deep sandy hollow, at the rear of 'The Chequers', a brick and timber ale house, halfway between Deal and Sandwich.

The skewbald carthorse munched contentedly on the over-grown grass next to the richly berried hedgerows. Jenny had tethered him to the free-standing wooden post that held the inn sign showing a black and white chess board.

A pair of linnets twittered and bounded over the dewy marram grass. Skylarks fluted and darted as they soared miles high overhead. In the distance a shepherd boy leaned against a derelict looker's hut and whistled shrilly to his companion, a shaggy sheepdog.

The pair were both concealed from the view of walkers and riders along the Ancient Highway. Yet, as a precaution, they kept their voices barely above a whisper. It was an unnaturally still morning. They guessed that even their hushed voices might carry through the waves of mist that still lingered over the sand dunes.

'Since when did you start working at the windmill?' queried Miles. 'You kept that mighty quiet! All the same, I'm rather glad you did!'

'A girl must keep some secrets,' chided Jenny. 'You seem to have found out most of ours.

And in a very short space of time!'

She picked the limp stalk of a late dandelion and held it under Miles' chin. 'This is to tell if you like butter,' she teased. 'It gives a yellow reflection if you do.'

Miles brushed it away.

'Country folk call them 'chimney sweepers',' Jenny informed. 'The seed heads, I suppose, look like brooms of chimney sweepers.' She twirled the dandelion round.

'I climbed the chimney in the 'Noah's Ark', as you know,' said Miles. 'Yet I still don't know how Jinx got into the tunnel. There must be another entrance. I'm guessing the chimney is an emergency exit. It wouldn't be convenient for anyone to climb it every time they needed to gain access into the roof space.'

'Perhaps there is. . . you will just have to keep looking!'

'Maybe you can show me, Jenny.' Miles picked at a strand of straw and ran it through his teeth. 'I am desperate to know. Where is it, please?'

'My grandmother, God bless her, used to say, 'Ask no questions and you'll be told no lies.'

She winked knowingly. 'That, for the time being, must suffice.'

Miles, who had proved to be a highly intelligent boy, had arrived in Deale with an enquiring mind and a determination to hunt out smugglers. This curiosity had brought him danger and excitement and not a little moral confusion. He had rapidly lost his shyness and reserve and gained confidence and courage. He would be a totally transformed youth once he returned, reluctantly, to London life.

'And there's one more thing that is troubling me. . . although I know now not to ask. I was just wondering how Miller Oakley manages to sell his flour so cheaply. I am just trying to puzzle out. . . in my own mind's eye, of course. . . where his money might actually come from.' He turned and gave a cheeky grin. 'I suppose none of this will have anything to do with his hiding smugglers in the boat cap of the windmill?'

'Hush, Miles! Bob down. Keep low. I think you are about to find out the answers to some of your questions right now. Look over there!'

They both lay on their stomach's and parted the long grass so they could peer between the gaps without themselves being seen. Figures were strangely silhouetted against the slate grey waters of the Small Downs. As the fragile sun burned through the mist, Miles and Jenny were able to witness the whole animated scene.

Lieutenant Gabriel Bray was patrolling a short distance offshore in his revenue cutter, 'Scorpion'. Presently, he boarded one of the boat's gigs with its modest crew, armed with swords and pistols, just as it was being lowered steadily into the water. The bosun took command of the vessel which was rowed - swiftly and silently - towards the shore, partly concealed by intermittent sea mist.

Their destination was a rambling timber warehouse close to the foreshore about a couple of miles from Sandown castle. It had been acquired by Miller Oakley who had repaired it only recently so that it would be dry and secure enough to store his grain. It had escaped being commandeered to billet troops for the obvious reason that the miller supplied flour, that much needed commodity, to the Dragoons. This rented warehouse had been left, unwisely, overlooked and completely alone.

'Follow me!' hissed Jenny. She seemed always now to take command. The pair ducked, dived and darted from one sand dune to another, taking great care to remain unobserved.

Zigzagging, they reached the beached wreck of a sailing barge to the right of the warehouse. It was partially buried in the sand with its ribs exposed to the elements. Through the cracks of its jagged timbers, they could see and hear with little difficulty.

Lieutenant Bray's focus of attention was upon the heavy warehouse doors that faced seawards. They were securely locked. Bray signalled to his men to break them down and search inside. For a time, these doors held but inevitably they buckled as they yielded to brute force. The true wares of the warehouse were about to be revealed.

Stacked high and dry from floor to rafters were scores of barrels chalked with their illegal contents - brandy, gin and rum. Perhaps of greater interest to the Lieutenant was the row of several sleek galleys. These were all twelve oared and highly illegal. Their purpose, to be sure, might easily be guessed.

Both boats and barrels were heavily guarded by burly, young boatmen. Stepping out from among them in the dark, gloomy interior was the slender figure of Thomas Oakley. Although unarmed, he remained resolute and fearless. He stood with his hands on his aproned hips, preparing to face the consequences of this clumsy ambush by the insufferable Lieutenant Bray.

'Who would have believed, Mr Oakley, that you were the ringleader of this ruffian gang?'

Bray's lips curled into a cruel smile. 'Pray, sir, you could hardly think that such a remote spot for a warehouse would not attract my vigilant attention! Even though it is under the very noses of the troops sent from Canterbury to investigate your illicit trade.' He spat on the ground to signify his contempt. 'Why chose such an accursed place to conceal your contraband?'

'The reason, Captain Bray, is simple,' Thomas Oakley replied with polite irony. 'The town is full of smuggled tea!'

'You, sir, are under arrest and your fleet is forfeit by the command of His Majesty King George.'

'First, Lieutenant Bray, you will need to capture me. . . and that may cause you quite a problem.'

Bray raised his pistol and aimed it directly at Thomas Oakley's forehead. 'Best come quietly, my good sir.'

Entirely on cue, the boatmen responded by rolling out a pair of carriage guns - loaded and primed - that had been hidden under piles of hessian flour sacks. They were pointing menacingly towards Bray's surprised officers.

'There is going to be a bloodbath,' whispered Miles.

'Then we must think of something to prevent it!' asserted Jenny.

The opposing sides - sailors and smugglers - faced each other across the lonely foreshore. Their confrontation was taking place directly in front of the miller's warehouse. It presented a sturdy structure with a steep roof that tilted towards the sea.

Its high back remained unprotected, unguarded.

'Maybe we could make a diversion if we climb onto the roof and somehow create an almighty din,' proposed Jenny. 'This might form a distraction that will allow Mr. Oakley and his men to make good their escape.'

'What again?' grumbled Miles. All the same he readily complied. After all, it was worth a try. By now, he was game for anything. . .

The intrepid pair dodged among the rippling sand dunes - sight unseen - until they arrived at the rear of the warehouse. There they found a pile of discarded nautical paraphernalia: lobster pots, driftwood, fishing nets, anchors, wooden crates. . .

'We could build some steps if we pile these crates on top of each other and make a platform with these pieces of driftwood laid across these broken barrels,' suggested Miles, breathlessly. He thought this was such a brilliant idea that straightaway he started to put it into practice by shifting a couple of heavy crates into position.

'How about if we just used this apple picker's ladder?' Jenny suggested. 'That's far more practical.'

Deflated, Miles helped Jenny retrieve the ladder from where it had been stored behind the crates. They then walked it carefully into position against the back wall of the warehouse.

'It's a bit narrow,' observed Miles. (He was peeved he hadn't spotted the ladder himself)

'You go first, and I'll follow,' offered Jenny. 'When you reach the top, I can shove you over the side and onto the roof.'

'Then what?' asked Miles, suspiciously.

'You make plenty of noise by jumping about on the timbers and banging together these tin cans. That will make everyone look up and perhaps buy some time. . . but be careful, the roof might not hold your weight.'

'Thank you for that,' granted Miles, sarcastically.

Miles scrambled up the bowed ladder with the cans. When he reached the top rung, he waited for Jenny to arrive behind him. Then she grabbed hold of his legs, extremely awkwardly, in an attempt to topple him over the high side of the warehouse. There he lay on his tummy staring down over the whole length of its alarming catslide roof.

'Can't you try and stand upright?' hissed Jenny, impatiently.

'I'm not there yet! I'll need one more push. Grab hold of my ankles.'

Jenny responded by pushing both of Miles' feet. Then the inevitable happened. As she gave that one last hefty heave it propelled the ladder backwards and she fell with a crash in a wide arc into prickly bushes. She was still clutching Miles' shoes!

At the same time Miles slid forwards - rumbling and tumbling - all the way down the long sloping roof, over the edge and down the front, rattling and clattering those tin cans.

Crash. . . bang. . . wallop.

He landed with a thump on his feet between the two sworn enemies - Miller Oakley and Lieutenant Bray.

For the second time in less than a week, Miles found himself looking down both barrels of a loaded pistol.

'This is where I came in!' he gasped as his vision started whirling and twirling before he completely. . . passed. . . out.

Stars and planets whizzed and whirled through Miles' head as he raised it from the bolster pillow. He experienced a bout of claustrophobia as he tried to make sense of his bearings. He was in a wooden bunk bed attached to one wall and enclosed by rich taffeta drapes.

He yawned, stretched and swished open the dainty curtains.

He was unprepared for the sight that greeted him. The room in which he had been sleeping - he had no recollection of how he got there - had low, broad beams and plain oak panelling. The sparse furniture consisted of a small writing desk, a slender corner chair and a substantial sailor's sea chest. There was a square of plain carpet to cover the bare boards. Light came from tallow candles with long shrouds in copper wall sconces, iron bound lanterns that hung from the ceiling and a fire that burned low in the grate with 'strangers' on the bar. A tilted mirror in the far corner reflected a slither of the new moon.

Above the mantlepiece was displayed a head and shoulders portrait of King George III. His Majesty was dressed in the uniform of a general. This consisted of a crimson coat with a black collar, gold epaulettes, buttons and braidings. A distinctive star and garter was pinned on his chest. An immense black feathered tricorn hat partially obscured a white, curled periwig. Majestically presented, the reigning monarch looked, for all the world, tired and troubled with daily life.

Plainly, Miles was in an Admiral's cabin on the upper gun deck of a first-rate ship of the line!

Miles slipped out of bed and skipped over to the tiny, patched-on bow window. He knelt on the battered chest and used his sleeve to rub a clear area in the grimy windowpane in order to peer out. The features he saw, though only half lit by the shy moon, were instantly recognisable. Directly below was the Downs Anchorage, behind were the Goodwin Sands and beyond them was the English Channel.

He guessed now that he was in the cabin on the top floor of Jenny's corner slop shop. She had taken him there herself before he passed out with sheer exhaustion. He realised, though, that this window provided the perfect look-out, seawards.

Maybe he should have further kept his wits about him as he perused the scene before him. He noticed, but failed to interpret, the steady build-up of shipping - Merchant and Royal Navy - entering the Downs from both directions - north and south - of the treacherous sandbank. This was always a tell-tale sign of a storm brewing in the English Channel.

Miles's mind, though, was on other things as he stared through the tiny windowpanes and tried to puzzle out the sequence of events that had brought him to this safe haven. Total confusion had reigned the moment he had landed in front of Thomas Oakley's warehouse. Lieutenant Bray had lowered his pistol - reluctantly, mind - and in that spilt second the former Mayor-cum-miller had dived behind the high stack of spirit barrels.

The crew of the gig ventured out from behind the row of wooden capstans that had been affording them cover and protection. They narrowly missed being blasted to smithereens by the shot from the carriage guns. When the smoke cleared there was no sign of any of the smugglers let alone the miscreant miller. . . just an irate Gabriel Bray, purple with rage.

The Lieutenant barked orders at his men to find Miller Oakley and his gang who had slipped out of a rear door and round the back of the warehouse. Immediately, they gave chase, but this was unknown territory and they soon lost him in the desolate, undulating dunes. Bray ordered his men to spread out and cover the entire Sandhills but eventually they had to admit they had lost their prey.

Coastal mist plays tricks, after all. . . Now you see him, now you don't . . .

Jenny retrieved the carthorse and untied him from the inn sign. She led him cautiously across the dunes towards the warehouse. Miles was sitting upright holding a bruised forehead. He allowed her to help him onto the back of the horse and lead him along the foreshore until they reached her home safely above the slops shop.

And he could remember Jenny saying firmly: 'They will be looking for you at the 'Ark', Miles. It's best you made yourself scarce for a time. We can keep you warm and safe where no one will think of searching for you.'

Miles was reflecting on Jenny's kindness and concern when something made him jump!

A face was staring back at him through the window glass. He felt foolish when he realised that the unfamiliar face was his own! It was pitch black outside so he could only guess the time. It must be either late afternoon, early evening or, possibly even dead of night.

Back in the present, Miles started to assess his dimly illuminated surroundings.

The oak panelling upon inspection was actually cheap, stained pine. . .

The embroidered bed hangings were merely hand painted sailcloth's. . .

The ornate mirror in the corner was severely cracked and foxed. . .

And the regal portrait was crudely painted and copied from a much-circulated painting at court. He had seen similar at several of the London mansions and country homes on social visits with his family. It did not quite ring true. . .

Here was a room that, at first glance, was most impressive and yet it was clearly designed to deceive.

That portrait, now, was a dead giveaway! Jenny and her boating companions were no royalists. They made their living by defying the law and evading justice. They robbed His Majesty's government of its imposed taxes to defend the country from invasion from France.

George III invited closer examination.

Miles moved the corner chair under the portrait. He stood on its seat and reached along the heavy frame. Yes. . . there it was. . . just as he expected. Towards the top of the portrait, he located an almost imperceptible catch. He pressed it hard and a whole wall panel shot forward to the right of the fireplace.

In the sudden draught the candles flickered, and the fire burned low.

There, revealed, was the cavernous store of contraband.

This, then was the true entrance to the smugglers' rooftop run. In the dark space beyond, Miles knew he would find stacks of kegs, packets of tobacco and crates of materials. All safely stored and secreted. He had no need to explore further.

Jinx meandered out. Proud and haughty. His sleek fur rose as he marched in front of the dying embers of the coal fire. There he was master of all he surveyed. He miaowed a contemptuous greeting before jumping onto the middle of the high bunk bed.

The disdainful cat allowed Miles to remove the loose collar of scallop shells from around his neck and place it over the finial of the wooden bedhead. Then Jinx turned round twice, settled himself down, folded his front paws under, as only cats can do, and promptly fell asleep.

Miles slipped once more under the blankets. He took care to arch his back as he wiggled down the bed so as not to disturb the dozing Jinx. Tentatively, he pulled the curtains across and shut out the night.

Wasn't there a saying. . . it went through Miles' mind as he drifted off to sleep. . . that it brought bad luck (yawn) if you happened to see a new moon (yawn) reflected in a looking glass?

10

STORM

JINX was balancing on the windowsill, his black fur stood on end and he was making long, low howls and growls. He hissed and he spat. He wailed like a banshee. Suddenly, he leaped down and dived behind the sea chest.

Miles was already wide awake. The whole room had begun to shake violently. It was icy cold and pitch black. The furniture rattled, the carpet lifted, and the wind whipped down the chimney. . .

'I'll huff and I'll puff, and I'll blow your house down. . .'

He climbed down from the bunk bed and felt his way across the room towards the latticed bow window. Rain was beating on the panes and a breeze was whistling through the bars. Although visibility was severely restricted, the horrendous noise and flashing lights told him of danger out at sea.

It was, indeed, blowing great guns.

At Sandown, the sails of Oakley's windmill swivelled round so violently that the friction of their spindle threatened to set the cap alight. The fate of this prize new mill was in further danger because, flour being highly combustible, the whole structure risked burning swiftly to the ground. The heavy windshaft dislodged in the gale and the four sails, still attached to their stocks, cartwheeled across the castle paddock and somersaulted into the swamped moat.

The military camp on the Sandhills was devastated. The wind tugged furiously on the guy ropes of the bell tents until they snapped while the flapping canvasses flew away like kites, leaving the sleeping soldiers exposed to full force of the hurricane. Terrified horses reared and bucked as they were led for safety from their makeshift stables for fear the roof might suddenly collapse.

The barn where the officers were billeted offered precious little shelter for it, too, was in danger of subsiding as the wind ripped through the timber planks. Captain Cannons made the decision to remove his entire regiment to the safety of Sandown Castle, no easy task when strong winds buckled the drawbridge and giant waves lashed the seaward walls.

Along the Ancient Highway, the executed pirate suffered yet further indignity as his body, clasped in the iron cage, spun round in the gale like a spinning top. Inevitably, its chain snapped so that both cage and occupant were flung out to sea where they vanished beneath freak waves for the remainder of eternity.

Further inland, trees in the churchyard were torn up by their roots and cast to the ground as if plucked by the hand of an ogre in a tantrum. Lead from the church roof likewise was rolled up like parchment and discarded in strips. The weathervane turned this way and that like a demented merry-go-round before its spindle splintered and speared to the ground. Its steeple also threatened to topple.

Mayor Powell experienced a narrow escape. His tall brick chimney crumpled and crashed through three floors exposing his private closet and part evidence of the secret rooftop run. Luckily, His Worship had already risen from his bed - which was completely crushed by falling masonry - and he rushed in his dressing gown to the foreshore to investigate the destruction of his beloved port. His concern for the welfare of the townsfolk saved his life.

All this Miles would learn of later. But for the present he witnessed the chaotic scene first-hand by pressing his nose against the grimy windowpanes. What he saw terrified him.

The Downs Anchorage was a scene of complete devastation. Ship after ship was ripped from its moorings and swept out to the open sea. Captains ordered hemp cables that held their anchors to be axed to prevent their vessels capsizing and also the mainmasts with torn canvasses to be toppled in order to avoid them careering out of control.

Such extreme endeavours were for the most part of little avail. For these massive ships still smashed into each other in the crowded anchorage where they were either sunk or driven towards the treacherous Goodwin Sands. The tempest did not discern between Royal or Merchant Navies. Both fleets suffered alike and their attendant vessels - transports, tenders, victualling and convict ships - were pounded together in an almighty melee.

Northwards, the recently installed North Goodwin lightvessel, although undulating violently, held fast to its iron cables and its triple oil lamps, or 'moon boxes', bobbed on their masts, warning of imminent danger from the concealed edges of the sandbanks.

These fearful images were witnessed by Miles through the raindrops streaming down the window and illuminated variously by ship's lanterns, distress rockets and sheet lightning.

Suddenly, a huge wave pounded the bow window and several panes of glass cracked.

Miles backed off in alarm and dived for cover under the blankets. He admitted to himself that he was afraid and there was no one on hand to help or comfort him. He felt helpless, confused and desperately alone in this bleak, vulnerable seaport.

Sleep evaded him because of the cacophony: the booming of the distress guns fired at minute intervals by ships in peril. . . the crashing of chimneys, turrets and towers of storm struck buildings. . . and the thunderclaps, seconds after each lightning flash, indicating the storm raged directly overhead. Miles tried hard to block out these sounds by pressing his hands over his ears. Above this tremendous noise and close at hand, Miles could discern a bell mournfully clanging. Its purpose posed a mystery.

It was midnight, a new moon and a spring tide.

'Mr Mayor! Mr Mayor!' Miles raced across the shingle and called out breathlessly. 'There are men on the Goodwins!' He handed over the spyglass he had borrowed from Jenny's father. 'Take a look for yourself, sir! I saw them from the upstairs window. They are trapped and doomed to die!'

Miles had been wakened by a tentative knock on the bedroom door. In came Jenny with a tray of bread and butter and a boiled egg, still with the hen's feather on its steaming shell, which she balanced on the bedclothes. Miles was surprised to find that he had fallen asleep after all. The last he remembered was listening to the distant thunder as it rolled around the coast and then returned, having lost only a little of its strength, to terrorise the gallant port.

Jenny explained, as she sat on the end of his bed, that she had been with her father and, indeed, most of the townsfolk, watching the storm half the night from the foreshore. She had acted promptly by running along the narrow alley alongside 'The Fountain Inn' where the Downs bell hung prominently on the high wall. She rang it vigorously to warn of danger out at sea and to summon aid, although she realised even at that time her swift action was hopeless. Everyone would be powerless to act in such a brutal tempest.

Miles felt guilty and ashamed that he had accepted the comfort of Jenny's kind hospitality. She had been braving the elements during that frightful night and yet she had not neglected him and had, in fact, returned purposely to prepare this welcome breakfast. He vowed that once he was home, he would never again allow any of his servants to wait on him or do anything that he might easily do for himself.

He joined Jenny and her father in their little parlour. The three of them stared out of the expansive bay window - careful to keep a short distance from the glass panes in case they caved in from flying debris - and surveyed the devastation. Miles was amazed how empty the beach was after the wind had swept it clean of rubble.

Banks of shingle completely covered the seafront road and surrounded the hulls of the repaired luggers hove high on the beach against the storm. It occurred to Miles these noble boats had been twice destroyed - first by fire and now by water. It was obvious, battered as they were, they would never again venture out to sea.

Jenny's father handed Miles the brass spyglass. It was heavy and he found it difficult to focus even when it was pointed out to him in which direction he should look. What he then saw through the thick lens horrified him. He did not hesitate but grabbed the spyglass and dashed out of the front door, battling to push it open against the wind. He darted among the milling crowd until he located Mayor Powell, now huddled in his shabby grogram coat.

'Turnabout, boy!' ordered Thomas Powell. Miles obeyed, still struggling to stand upright against the whipping wind while the Mayor rested the heavy spyglass on his right shoulder. Meticulously, the Mayor scanned the horizon. He allowed the cloudy lens to sweep past the carnage in the Downs until he finally focused on a huddle of men, frantically waving their torn shirts and running desperately across the raised northern bank of the Goodwins.

Meanwhile, Lieutenant Bray and his officers were themselves busy on the beach. They showed little concern, however, for the sailors still stranded out at sea. Instead, they wandered to and fro along the foreshore - despite the high wind and heavy rain - investigating the contents of wooden crates washed ashore. And making sure that none of the boatmen were able to spirit away anything they contained that might be of value.

Deale has a long beach, however, and it was impossible for Bray's men to cover the whole three miles of exposed coastline. Boatmen also tramped and traipsed along the shingle at low water, oblivious of the stinging spray. They were strangely attired - baggy oilskin trousers that reached up to their armpits, coats fastened with ropes that covered their knees, heavy cloth jackets buttoned closely over their blue woollen jerseys, long knitted scarves or 'mufflers' wound tightly round their neck and 'sou-wester' with flaps that prevented the driving rain from trickling down their back - against this foul weather.

These boatmen were themselves intent on apportioning anything that might offer the possibility of resale before the return of the boisterous tide. They strolled back and forth, heads down, searching the same section of beach over and over again. They skilfully dodged the boiling surf as it scoured away enormous chunks of sand and shingle. They laughed when they became splattered with spray and chuckled when they alighted upon something of possible worth. They seemed impervious to the elements.

The items that lay upon the shore were many and varied - kegs of gunpowder, packs of musket flints, boxes of candles. . . Most important was the amount of seasoned timber thrown up that would be most useful to the boatmen when rebuilding their seaside homes. Traditionally, all these objects were regarded as 'findalls.'

The plucky Mayor, nothing afraid, stormed over to Lieutenant Bray and confronted him. Miles followed at a distance. This meant he could hear only snatches of their conversation as it was blown towards him by the gusting wind.

'Leave that, Lieutenant! . . . Turn your face, if you will, to the sea. . . There are brave sailors. . . stranded out there on the Sands. . . that need your assistance.'

Lieutenant Bray's reply was lost to Miles, yet he could tell by his defiant stance that he was determined to ignore the plight of the marooned seamen. Miles edged a little closer to the two sparring gentlemen. The driving rain stung his face like splinters of glass, and he was soaked all the way through to his underclothes.

'There is no way these boatmen can rescue them,' bellowed the red-faced Mayor, as he poked his finger repeatedly into the Lieutenant's puffed-up chest. 'As you are perfectly well aware, all their boats have been destroyed, not by this storm but by the direct orders of Mister Pitt. They require immediate access to your own fleet stowed, I believe, in the Customs House.'

'My boats,' spelled out the irate Lieutenant, 'remain safely under lock and key for the obvious reason. . . that they will be severely damaged if they venture forth in a hurricane force wind. I cannot take the risk that they too may be completely destroyed.'

'You, sir, are a fool and a coward!' retorted the Mayor, shaking the Lieutenant vigorously by his shoulders. He could hardly contain his fury as he spat out his contempt for this stubborn naval officer. 'Boats may be safe in a harbour, Lieutenant, but that's not what boats are built for!'

Enraged, Mayor Powell turned to Miles. He fumbled under his coat and pulled out a leather drawstring purse. He tipped the contents into Miles' frozen hands and ordered him to distribute the tinkling, jingling gold coins among the boatmen. 'Offer these to any of them who will dare to venture forth to the Goodwin Sands.'

Immediately there was a flurry of activity on the beach. A large group of boatmen gathered round the Mayor. They recognised his leadership and responded to his authority. They were willing to obey his every order which was both direct and decisive.

The Mayor continued to take charge of the situation. He ordered a group of strong men to lift a heavy bowsprit cast up upon the beach and carry it on their broad shoulders in the direction of the Custom House. This sturdy brick build building had withstood the brunt of the storm and remained undamaged apart from a few roof tiles that had been shattered.

The boatmen knew instinctively what was required of them. Pocketing the gold guineas, they attacked the locked double doors robustly, employing the bowsprit as a battering ram.

Thud. . . thud. . . THUD. . .

Inevitably, the timber doors began to splinter and shatter. Soon the men gained access to the interior of the boatshed. There stood a number of impounded galleys alongside one magnificent lugger, recently confiscated from the Deale boatmen by Lieutenant Bray.

This was that notorious smuggling vessel, 'Diana', which, when apprehended by Revenue Men just as she was returning under the White Cliffs, was found to contain an enormous consignment: casks of Dutch gin, brandy, rum and countless bottles of fine French and Spanish wine. This vast cargo of illicit spirits inspired one wit to remark that she was more afloat inside than out!

'Now my lads, it is your responsibility to man these boats,' thundered the Mayor. 'You must aim directly for the North Sands.' Then he offered this firm assurance, 'Every one of you will be amply rewarded for your labours but first and foremost you will have the satisfaction that the lives of honest sailors will be saved.'

In the scramble for places, Miles found himself being picked up roughly by the shoulders once more and this time flung over the high gunwale onto the deck of the infamous lugger. 'You, too, laddie', cried his assailant hoarsely. 'We are all in this - man and boy - together!'

❦

'Diana' was straining on her slip chain as Miles was hauled aboard. Her bow was already pointing seawards in readiness for an immediate launch - at any time of the day or night.

Her hastily recruited crew consisted of about half a dozen boatmen from the rowdy crowd. They swiftly donned cork life-jackets in preparation for their hazardous mission. One of them thrust a jacket across to Miles and then helped him to secure it around his body. He recognised the man as Sam Harris. They exchanged a wry smile. Everything happened so quickly that Miles found no time to be alarmed.

After all, this was to be the start of an awfully big adventure.

An assortment of eager Deale folk had hastily assembled on the beach in front of the Custom House. They were mainly elderly folk - men and women - but a few of the local children arrived to lend a hand. Old or young, everyone seemed familiar with the firmly established routine of launching a lugger. They positioned the greased wooden skids in a straight line down the sloping beach by using the attached strong coiled ropes. Miles thought he could glimpse Jenny in the crowd, but he couldn't be sure.

'Hold tight!'

Miles gripped the rough timber stern thwart on which he was perched precariously with both hands and watched his knuckles whiten as he waited with bated breath for the dramatic launch.

An experienced beach hand stood poised to unhook the

slip chain the moment he judged there to be the briefest lull in those relentless, thrashing waves. After a brief few seconds of comparative calm the taut chain was released. The mighty lugger thundered down the steeply sloping beach, gathering momentum as she rumbled over the skids and careered into the frothy breakers.

The thrill of the descent was awesome. Miles screamed - he felt ashamed - but thankfully no sound was heard above the roar of the mighty storm. Luckily, his dignity remained intact.

The skipper - John Atkins - adjusted the winter rigging the instant the lugger left the open shore. This was a tough task in an unruly wind. A great parchment coloured dipping sail was hoisted halfway up the foremast while the mizzen - positioned well aft - was already equipped with its standing 'lug' and a topsail. In addition, a massive storm jib was drawn out along the long bowsprit. Even in ordinary circumstances, this amount of canvas would send the boat way ahead and to the windward of the fastest ship that dared to compete against it.

The lugger responded and chased through the blustery sea. Icy spray flew over the gunwales and stung the boatmen's ruddy faces. Miles turned his head momentarily into the wind to watch the receding shoreline. It was a distressing sight that he glimpsed.

The storm had wreaked havoc with the landscape. The telegraph tower of the Navy Yard had tumbled, and the cupola of St George's Church had crashed. Northwards, Sandown windmill stood bereft of cap and sails and the exposed military camp on the Sandhills had clearly borne the brunt of the storm.

Along the coast the boatmen's slipways, capstans, stages, sheds and flagpoles had received a terrific pounding. As he turned his head once more to avoid the constant pain from wind and spray, Miles acknowledged that nature can never, ever be tamed.

Not one man spoke for it was impossible to be heard above the roaring of the wind, the whistling of the rigging and the cracking of the sails. Miles could hardly breathe let alone speak. But it was obvious, even without enquiring, that they were heading directly towards the northern extremity of the Goodwins, driven by that wild, south westerly wind.

Skipper Atkins was careful to keep the distant North Goodwin lightvessel to starboard. He had great difficulty establishing his bearings because only those three castles - Walmer, Deale and Sandown - remained as visible seamarks on the battered shore. Stone built; they could withstand the most vicious storm, but they had also been deliberately positioned low on the horizon. This was to avoid being targets of cannon fire from hostile French ships who dared to invade this vulnerable corner of Kent.

Ahead, there was the constant danger from floating wreckage - 'flotsam' - and jettisoned cargo - 'jetsam' - from storm damaged vessels that raced past in the fast-running sea. These consisted of masts, spars, rudders, tillers, even a ship's wheel that normally the crew would attempt to salvage along with sunken anchors and cables. Here and now, though, the men were concerned by the immense damage that might be caused should anything strike the steep hull of their lugger.

'Youngster!' ordered Will Norris. 'Move over to the cuddy - that cabin at the bow - and keep a sharp look out for debris.' This was shouted with cupped hands directly into Miles' frozen face. The boy nodded that he understood. He eagerly obeyed by tumbling forward across the swaying deck, climbing onto the forward thwart and grabbing hold of the samson post that secured the cable for an anchor. 'Point out anything that comes towards us… and KEEP pointing till we have dealt with it!'

George Rands joined William Norris - one at starboard, the other larboard - ready with stout oars poised to push away any obstacle that came bearing down on 'Diana'.

Skipper Atkins, throughout the tortuous voyage, was constantly checking the strength and direction of the wind and keeping a sharp eye on how his sails were set. The westerly wind, coming directly from the land, was assisting the lugger speed towards the north bank while the low ebbing tide was pulling the boat in the opposite direction towards the south bank of the Goodwins.

Fortunately, he was experienced in dealing with this conflict of helping wind and hindering tide. At one time, though, he was forced to order Sam Harris to 'reef the sails' in order to improve the boat's stability and reduce the risk of capsizing. The great danger, of course, was that too much canvas in such a strong wind might result in the gallant rescuers being tipped, themselves, into the seething cauldron!

After what seemed to Miles an eternity battling against the elements, 'Diana' approached the western edge of the North Goodwin Sands.

Skipper Atkins, assessing the wind and tide, was confident that he could strike the sails and lower the anchor. His crew sighed relief at their safe arrival close to the highest point of the sandbank, marked on charts as 'Jamaica Land.' (Miles stared ahead and thought that the landscape bore precious little resemblance to his schoolroom textbook depictions of blue mountains, palm trees, sapphire seas and sugary sands on that paradise Caribbean island.)

The Goodwins shift with every turn of the tide. This makes them nigh impossible to chart with accuracy. Mainly, they lie submerged beneath the waves in the middle of the world's busiest seaway, the English Channel. Twice every day they are revealed and at each low tide they swiftly harden in even the briefest spell of sunshine.

Even on calm days it is difficult to get one's bearings from the distant silhouette of misty coastlines beyond the low, scudding clouds. There will be little sign of the wrecks of ships apart from a few submerged hulls and stubborn masts that are being engulfed for they quickly disappear forever, almost at the rise of the next tide.

Skipper Atkins had every reason to play safe. He could not fail to notice the number of recent wrecks that were sinking fast into the ravenous sands. Luggers were built with a shallow draught that enabled them to sail over the treacherous sand-bank in just a few feet of water at high tide. He determined; however, he was not going to risk his crew becoming further casualties by drawing in too close while the Sands were being beaten by strong winds and lashed by high waves. Wisely, he had moored a safe distance from where he could see the stranded sailors starting to assemble.

They were ragged. . . they were starving. . . they were exhausted. Above all they were terrified. Relief, they must surely realise, was close at hand. . . but they were in a state of shock that they could barely take in that fact. They struggled to stand upright against the biting wind and rubbed their eyes, caked with particles of flying sand. They huddled in a tight group at the top of a steep slope that slid down towards the lugger which was to be their salvation.

Miles watched as Will Norris uncoiled a thick rope and passed it over to George Rands. He tied one end to the mizzen mast and the other to a keg which he flung over the side.

Miles was intrigued. He lent over the gunwale of the violently swaying lugger to see what would happen next.

Inevitably, the wind and tide carried the keg with the rope attached through the whizzing, whirling maelstrom towards the stranded men. It washed ashore and the crew waited for the men to respond. These were seasoned sailors but none of them could swim - few bothered to learn in those callous times for if they fell overboard, they wanted a swift demise as their ship sailed on - and they froze in fear at the thought of wading through those treacherous waters.

Eventually, one of the sailors entered the water and grabbed hold of the rope. He knew he was to take a turn at steadying it while his partner used it to guide him through the thrashing foam to safety. The first man walked only a few paces while struggling to keep his balance before relying on the taut rope to lead him towards his rescuers.

The Sinking Sands - true to their fearful reputation - were reluctant to release their grip of their victim's feet but as the water became deeper the sailor was able to half float while laboriously passing his hands repeatedly over the rope. Hand over hand. . . over hand. . . over hand.

After what seemed like hours but in reality, was probably only minutes the spent sailor reached the lugger. Two boatmen lent over and lifted him aboard. None of the crew had either strength or energy left to cheer.

Encouraged by their companion's success, the remaining sailors followed suit. One by one by one. In this manner, almost all the stranded sailors were hauled to safety.

Immediately, they were covered with coarse woollen blankets fetched from within the cuddy and laid down in the bottom of the boat on a pile of crisp, dry oilskins. They were offered brandy and bread to warm and nourish them. Unable to summon the strength to speak they smiled and nodded their gratitude.

There was only one sailor left now on the sandbank. He had been left holding the rope and he was reluctant to leave. Miles could see why.

At his side was a soggy wet bundle that shivered and shook. It howled and whined and barked. Its face looked up intently at his owner who appeared even more bedraggled than his scraggy companion. Its look signalled confidence and trust. Miles knew at once that its master would never abandon his faithful hound even if it meant exposing his own life to acute danger.

'It's the ship's mascot!' mouthed Miles. 'A dog!'

Sam Harris kicked off his boots and knocked off his sou'wester. He climbed onto a thwart and dived over the side. He strove manfully through the water until he struggled onto the exposed sands.

Pushing the hesitant sailor ahead of him, he waited until he had reached the lugger safely, before releasing the rope from the barrel and tying it around his own waist.

Then he grabbed the mongrel by the scruff of its neck and allowed his crew members to haul them both back to the lugger. The dog paddled frantically but managed to keep its snout above the water. Finally, the crew hauled Sam Harris and the dog aboard 'Diana'.

Miles hugged the drenched animal as it settled down beside him on the thwart. First, though, it turned around and shook itself vigorously so that the entire crew were once more splattered with salt spray! The dog reminded Miles - just a little - of his own pampered pet, Lucy. Its bright eyes twinkled, and his rough tongue licked his face in gratitude. For the first time on that eventful voyage Miles and all his companions laughed.

Secretly, Miles had renewed admiration for Sam Harris, a convicted smuggler who had faced transportation, for risking his own life to save a scraggy hound. Most definitely, he had replaced Captain Cannons, as a role model, in his mind for bravery and integrity.

'All aboard!'

For some while, Skipper Atkins allowed 'Diana' to ride at anchor. He was waiting for the inevitable return of the young flood tide. When it came the wind began to abate and the sea became calmer. The crew began to fix their oars in the rowlocks and braced themselves for the long haul, rowing landwards, towards the Kentish shore.

Ensign reversed as a sign of distress, the valiant Deal lugger 'Diana', finally departed. Homeward bound.

Miles looked down from the gunwales as the sea began to cover the shoals. He noticed that peculiar phenomena of whirlpools in the shallow water near the sandbank and, curiously, seawater not just racing over the edge but forcing its way upwards - fast and furious - through the soft sand.

Before his very eyes, he watched mesmerised as that legendary leviathan, the Goodwin Sands, breathed its last few moments before vanishing once more beneath the waters of the English Channel.

🐚 🐚 🐚

A mysterious stranger entered the 'Noah's Ark' about mid-morning the day after the storm. He was shabbily dressed in a worn, torn overcoat with a tattered, battered hat. Under his drab grey topcoat there were flashes of an embroidered silk waistcoat and a jewelled pin in his stock.

'Landlord, if you please, a seat by your fire and a pint of your best!'

Pulling off, with great difficulty, his calf length boots, he first warmed his stockinged feet by the fire before sitting down at a convenient table. He produced a small writing slope and fumbled inside for a quill pen and a travelling inkpot. He dabbed water drops from his ample side whiskers with a silk kerchief and placed on his bulbous nose a pair of gold rimmed spectacles. He looked around the room and gave an approving smile.

He then took out a sheet of paper, dipped his quill in ink and poised to scribble.

Lew Bristowe, like everyone else in the town, had risen before dawn to survey the damage to his property. He mounted a long ladder and started to sweep the debris from the gutters and then looked with alarm at the replaced inn sign hanging precariously on just one hinge. He went across the street to help his neighbour pump out water from his cellar. Splinters of glass littered the street and there were fragments of broken chimney pots everywhere.

He was working hard when a troop of dragoons rode along Middle Street, their horses picking their way gingerly among these sharp obstacles. Captain Cannons, leading his men, looked neither to the right nor to the left, blinkered as his mount. The military camp on the Sandhills had been devastated - the hired barn collapsed, bell tents blown away, even the iron cooking pot had bowled like a cannon ball over the marram grass.

Before they could begin their own repairs, express orders had been received from Prime Minister William Pitt. The Dragoons from Canterbury were to be deployed from catching smugglers to guarding the cliffs at Dover and Folkestone. It was imperative, the orders stressed, to protect the coast against the French who might take the opportunity of the hazardous weather to invade east Kent.

Then, the stranger had arrived. Huffing and puffing, wheezing and sneezing. He hurried along the street with a wooden writing box under his arm, entered the inn and promptly made himself at home.

'It has taken me four hours to walk over from Dover. Four hours, would you believe? I thought I would never get here! It was like an assault course! The way is almost completely blocked. Drafted troops are out mending the road from Dover to Canterbury. To allow the mail coaches through, you understand. And that is where I must send my copy.'

Lew placed the tankard of frothy ale in front of his customer, pocketed the silver fourpence he had thrown onto the table in ample payment and waited for a further explanation of his intriguing business.

'I am, landlord, a reporter!'

Uncle Lew, sensing publicity for his business, summoned up upon the instant a group of boatmen who were eager to give an account of their additional exploits in the horrendous storm. They gathered excitedly around the journalist who listened intently and recorded their statements. They were thrilled by the possibility that their name (which, since none of them could read or write, would recognise) might appear in print.

Flies around the honeypot.

John Atkins, the stranger learned, had dived from the comparative safety of the lugger into the frenzied waters to rescue an exhausted midshipman clinging to a mast.

Will Norris employed a grappling iron to secure a makeshift raft with three terrified sailors and the ship's cat precariously aboard.

George Rands had swum out from the beach into the rough sea with a rope attached to his waist and fastened it to a laden galley for his comrades to haul ashore.

Sam Harris laughed as he told how his oilskins were so stiff with ice that when he pulled them off, they stood up on their own accord!

Truly, these were newsworthy tales of extreme bravery.

Even Goggin's fickle sweetheart, Nancy, tempted by the chance of momentary fame, skipped over to relate how she had dashed out from the 'Three Mariners' in the middle of the night, without stopping to put on her best fur coat or even her expensive jewellery, to hold a greased skid for one of the luggers and that she had soiled her best kid gloves, given to her by a former admirer as a keepsake, and she had so loved him at the time, yet in all the flurry of activity she hadn't, she simply hadn't once, not once, complained. Everyone, in a whirlwind of generosity, agreed that she had indeed played a most important part in the recent dramas.

The boatmen's only financial reward, they let slip in hushed whispers, was that they managed to salvage a few crates of sugar, tea, tobacco and uncorked champagne which they would keep secret from the Revenue Officers. These they regarded as their deserved 'perks'.

'This', declared the reporter confidently, 'is bound to make the front page of tomorrow's newssheet, 'The Mermaid's Locker', and perhaps - who knows? - it might even make the broadsheets of the London coffee houses.

Everyone murmured their approval.

Attracted by all the commotion, the rescued mongrel appeared from behind the counter, approached the stranger tentatively, growled and retreated, much to the amusement of the company.

Miles padded downstairs still rubbing the sleep from his eyes. He had returned to the inn after his adventure and had decided he had earned 'a little lie in'. . . He picked his way through several exhausted boatmen still dozing on the floor of the passage. He was not, himself, wide awake but was hoping to find a warming drink and a bite to eat as he entered the taproom. There, he was surprised to find a noisy crowd gathered around a scholarly visitor, writing at a table, making detailed notes.

The crowd parted as Miles approached. 'This is my nephew', announced Lew proudly to the respectable gentleman. 'He will have his own tale to tell you. An exciting one, at that!'

Disdainfully, the respectable gentleman merely brushed Miles with his eyes. He sniffed. Clearly, he was thinking whatever could a common boatboy tell him that could be of any interest? He sneered. The lad was dirty, grubby and, upon my word, decidedly dishevelled. He snorted. He brushed his tousled hair and blew his bulbous nose.

Aunt Gwen pushed Miles forward. She put down the stone jug of milk that had turned sour after the storm. 'This is a reporter from Canterbury. Tell him what you did and how brave you were. You might find your name in the newspapers.'

'I don't think I care to,' Miles responded, petulantly.

'Now why ever would you say that?' Aunt Gwen reproached him. 'Tell this kind gentleman what part you played. He's written down all our names and our stories.'

'So I can see. . .'

A look of panic swept across the reporter's face. His wolfish eyes belied his sheepish grin. He had been struck by a terrible thought. The boy could read!

'DEALE SHARKS'. . . 'COWARDLY CONDUCT'. . . 'RUTHLESS WRECKERS.'

Boldly and deliberately, Miles read aloud, then pointed to the startling banner headline:

'CARNAGE IN THE CUT-THROAT TOWN OF DEALE.'

Everyone in the room froze. They realised in that moment they were being betrayed. The reporter was blatantly misrepresenting them. He was not concentrating on their heroic deeds. There was not one mention of their courageous exploits! He was denouncing them for their meagre plunder. It dawned on the company then of the old adage: 'Scandal sells.'

Lew Bristowe was the first to act. He swept the writing slope across the table. He hurled the inkpot across the room. He screwed up the paper and threw it into the fire. The last thing he did was to hurl the calf length boots at the terrified reporter as he made a hasty retreat out of the inn door.

The splendid travelling chariot with its match pair of horses drew up directly outside the 'Noah's Ark' where it attracted quite a crowd. Men envied, boys whistled, women wowed. Everyone was used to fine carriages, attended by their owner's obedient Dalmatians, whisking past on these narrow, cobbled streets. Hardly ever did they think to turn their head at the plod of hooves, the creak of leather or the jingle-jangling of harness bells.

But this. . . this was a gem of a vehicle!

The proud postillion - he hated being called a 'postboy' - waited patiently, mounted on the nearside horse, holding the reins of the superior black drawing horses. He had pulled the wide brim of his leather hat over his eyes to avoid being stared at by this inferior crowd. He felt uncomfortable in this humble seaside town and preferred the experience of driving his master and mistress along fashionable Chiswick Mall.

The spanking new chariot parked outside the inn had been customised for speed, comfort, luxury and, definitely, opulence. Its sleek jet black and light blue body was supported on leather cee springs to cushion privileged occupants travelling long distances on stony roads while its slim iron wheels lifted the carriage high to allow them uninterrupted views of the surrounding countryside.

There were further refinements. Oil lamps and door handles were solid brass, the windows were fitted with panes of glass and - should anyone dare to stand on tiptoe and peep inside - the double forwards facing seat was upholstered in padded pale blue leather. Of particular interest to all and sundry was an exquisite butterfly painted in gold on the two door panels. This was the distinctive crest of the Papillons.

Monsieur Papillion, exquisitely retired in a mulberry cut away coat, had safely returned from his precarious expedition to the Continent. Declining to enlist in the service of General Bonaparte, he had consequently forfeited his considerable lands in Montpelier. After travelling across the whole of France, he had stolen an open fishing boat to row himself across the English Channel.

Disguised as a citizen peasant he had sewn portable family heirlooms, including precious jewels, in his underclothes. He had landed under the cliffs at Folkestone and ridden overland on hired horses across Kent until he reached London.

The only visible sign of his escapades was a small black silk patch across his cheek to disguise the scar from a random pistol wound.

Monsieur Papillion was now anxious to be reunited with his shy, young son and to return him to their family mansion in the remote riverside village of Chiswick.

Earlier, Miles had been tucking into a hearty late breakfast - bacon, sausages, tomatoes, mushrooms, kidneys - all fresh from the kitchen stove! He ate freshly baked huffkins with thickly spread butter. He swallowed a third cup of strong, steaming coffee. He couldn't believe how hungry he was!

Aunt Gwen watched him attentively from across the trestle table covered with a crisp laundered tablecloth. 'You mustn't forget to write,' she prompted for the umpteenth time, although, in truth, she had never learned to read. 'I've packed you some sandwiches for the journey,' she fussed. 'And an apple and some dates.'

Uncle Lew came over from the counter and handed Monsieur Papillon a bottle of brandy. 'Best keep it hidden.' He winked and added warmly, 'I'm proud of my young nephew.'

Miles stood up and offered a slight bow. He had changed into his normal city clothes, but they felt stiff and starch. This was something that he had never before noticed.

'Turn round,' said Aunt Gwen. She linked the chain of the gold locket around his neck. 'You must keep this well and truly hidden on your journey home.' She tucked the precious heirloom behind the high collar of Miles' powder blue peacoat. Then turned him back and gave him one big sloppy kiss.

Miles surveyed his image in the smeared looking glass above the crackling fire. He wiped the signs of his aunt's kiss from his cheek using his lace shirt sleeve. He cut quite a dash for such a young gentleman. He allowed himself a satisfying smile. For once in his short life, he had actually won the approval of his country relatives. They had made him feel a true hero.

All the same he felt confused. He had come to Deale in search of smugglers. He had intended denouncing them. Instead, he had befriended them and protected them. He knew he would have to keep this association a secret from his own family. He was not sure that he would feel comfortable doing that. The plain truth was that he had discovered the whole town, including perhaps his aunt and uncle, was somehow involved in the 'Midnight Trade'.

Miles bade his farewells. His father lifted him up into the vehicle. The postillion hallooed and they were on their way.

Skilfully, the horses negotiated the tight street corner and trotted confidently towards the seafront.

Tears, waves and one or two smiles.

The travelling chariot halted at the top of Silver Street. Jenny was standing on the high stone step of the corner shop. She was holding Jinx awkwardly in her folded arms. 'We've both come to wish you a safe journey.'

Miles leaned out of the carriage and ruffled the fur on Jinx's head. In response, the cat gave a startled miaow. Then he sprang out of his mistress's arms and raced down the cobbled street. The last Miles saw of his feline friend was a long, rough tail, wagging crossly.

'Miles, when you remember, you must send your fine

carriage to collect me!' prompted Jenny. 'Don't forget, your promise. You must introduce me to London's High Society. One day, I vow, I shall be a fine lady!'

'I think you are one already,' responded Miles.

This time it was Jenny's turn to blush. She did a mock courtesy. It seemed the moment for an exchange of gifts.

'Close your eyes and hold out your hand,' Miles ordered.

Jenny found a small, hard, round object pressed into her palm. It was a crinkly walnut shell. She prized open the shell with her thumbnails and from inside she unfolded an exquisite pair of white silk gloves.

'Wherever. . .?' Jenny began but stopped herself in amazement.

'Ask no questions. . .' whispered Miles.

Jenny gave Miles a dainty kiss on his forehead. 'And here's something to remind you of your friends at the seaside.' This time it was her turn to fold a tiny gift into Miles's cupped hand.

'All right - ya hip!' cried the postillion and the chariot sped away!

Miles popped his head back inside as it was driven along the foreshore. Boatmen paused as they shifted their repaired wrecked luggers back onto their allotted stations. They raised their caps and waved heartily.

Mayor Powell stood among them, generous to a degree, still doling out gold guineas towards the cost of repairing these celebrated boats, employed in daring rescues. He, too, raised his cocked hat - this time revealing a cheap squirrel wig - as a fond farewell.

Before he pulled up the window Miles Papillion took a last long look at the now familiar beach at Deale.

All was calm and quiet. Waves lapped gently on the foreshore at this lowest of tides as if to deny all knowledge and responsibility of the recent maritime catastrophe. Small boats riding at anchor bobbed and curtsied elegantly while their flags and pennants fluttered and waved politely to persons on the shore.

The sea, however, was still littered with wreckage: keels of unidentifiable craft floating uppermost. . . broken masts sticking out of the water at peculiar angles. Ships' timbers and tangled canvas floating on the water were further evidence of the devastation caused by the late, great tempest.

As he held Jenny's present of a whelk shell to his ear Miles could distinctly hear above the thunder of the horses' hooves and the clattering of the coach wheels the persistent sound of the sea. . .

. . . and if he had cared to look back through the tiny square glass aperture in the rear of the plush travelling chariot, he would have noticed the heavy clouds parting to reveal a rainbow spreading. . . magically. . . across the busy town and still waters of the renowned Downs Anchorage.